AFTERSHOCKS

Erin Wilkerson

This is a work of fiction. Names, characters, businesses, places, events, locales, and incidents are either the products of the author's imagination or used in a fictitious manner. Any resemblance to actual persons, living or dead, or actual events is purely coincidental.

ISBN-13 Paperback: 979-8994829615
Amazon ASIN: B0GPQ74NGP

Cover and Artwork by:
Jasmine Bolting: twentyonepixelarts@outlook.com
Judah Lamey / Glint of Mischief: https://www.glintofmischief.com/
Inteerior formatting by Melody Kepler: www.keplerpstudios.com

Author website: https://authorerinwilkerson.com/
Publisher website: www.keplerpstudios.com

To my mother, who gifted me a love of reading

And to my father, who gifted me a love of Sci Fi.

Six years before
The Disaster

Twelve-year-olds are idiots.

Not because they are loud or mean or had questionable hygiene—that's standard issue.

They're idiots because they think life gets better.

River was all too aware he was one of them, as Vincent bragged about the new designer shoes his mommy bought him. Shoes that cost more than most families made in a month. This walking participation trophy waved them around like they were forged by gods and not stitched together by underpaid interns with a glue gun and a bad caffeine addiction.

River almost pitied him. Almost.

Adulthood: that uninvited guest that kicked down your door, ate all your cereal, and crushed your soul into fine collagen powder, like the overpriced kind Vincent's mom kept in a glass jar labeled *Vitality*.

He scanned the aluminum bleachers, row after row of adults at a gym competition, slumped like laundry, faces lit by phones or dulled by resignation. He searched for one face, *just one*, still clinging to a flicker of joy.

Nothing. Just hollowed expressions of souls that bartered

their wonder away for mortgages, PTA meetings, and wine-fueled dinner parties with people they hated.

And no carefully curated childhood, no organic snacks, no screen-time limit enforced by an exhausted therapist was going to save Vincent, or any of them from the reality ahead.

Maybe River was broken.

Or maybe he was the only one paying attention.

"Nice dismount, Derek," River said, not even bothering to mask the smirk as his teammate was ushered past him toward the cool-down zone

He hadn't even bothered watching the routine. Didn't need to.

Derek always tanked the landing.

The kid whipped around. "Shut it, River," he snapped, before a volunteer herded him away.

River cupped his hands and called after him, loud enough for the whole team to hear. "And your form was about as tight as Vincent's mom after spin class."

Vincent let out a strangled squeal. "Hey! What are you saying about my mom?" He glanced around like an ostrich catching the scent of a lion—confused, concerned, vaguely majestic.

"Think hard, Butterball," River said. "You'll get there someday."

Then came the call.

His turn. *Finally.*

He exhaled and rolled his shoulders, stepping onto the runway. Bright lights bore down, harsh and hot, illuminating every flaw.

The loudspeaker crackled. "River Sarcosa. On vault."

Goosebumps prickled his arms. The applause was polite, hollow. None of them even knew him.

He didn't move. Just stood at the edge, letting the silence stretch, letting them wait. Sweat beading on his brow already.

The sensations lit him up from the inside. Brought him to

life.

Eyes shut, he ran the sequence through in his mind. Sprint. Round-off. Springboard. Handspring. Twist. Flip. Land.

Then he ran.

He stuck the landing. Near perfect. The crowd erupted.

River scrunched his nose. That flip was garbage. They'd cheer for anything.

A volunteer slipped a gold medal over his head. River examined it: cheap and meaningless. His father paid two thousand dollars a month—for this?

The other medalists were hugged, cheered, and photographed by proud parents. River only had Ted. His stone-faced chauffeur-slash-bodyguard waiting by the door.

River stepped off the podium, walked past the snack table, and dropped the medal in the trash without slowing down.

The ride home was dead quiet. Unlike the last guy, Ted didn't try to talk to him.

That's why River liked Ted.

At home, he slipped quietly through the kitchen, ignored by the busy staff, following to the main hall of white columns, burgundy tapestries, and polished floors echoing with emptiness. He traced the carved swirls of the mahogany banister.

And stopped halfway up.

His father stood there, arms crossed. Glaring.

Today was River's birthday, but he doubted very much that was why his father graced him now with his presence. The man had always despised him, but as River grew smarter—stronger. It's only gotten worse.

"Did you throw a cinder block off the roof onto Hunter's sports car?" his father growled.

Of course he did. The guy was a total douche canoe.

River crossed his arms, keeping calm. "Define *throw*." It was more of a shove. Cinderblocks are heavy.

His father's nostrils flared. "Don't get cute with me. That over-gelled possum is threatening to sue."

River rolled his eyes. “He drove into Mia, breaking her leg. Then you fired her for missing work.” Mia had been the only person in this pathetic world River could stand. And now she was gone.

His father stepped closer. “I'm also missing a two-million-dollar watch. That you, too?”

River shrugged, looking away. “Slipped it into Mia’s purse when the ambulance took her.”

His father sighed, dialing his phone. “Maury, I'm in the hall.”

A minute later, Maury appeared.

“Call the police. Tell them a former housekeeper stole my watch,” his father ordered.

River’s stomach dropped. “You'll get her deported!”

His father crouched to eye level. “Maybe you'll finally learn to stop touching my things.”

“But you have thirty! You wouldn’t miss one.”

“That's not the point. Get upstairs. Play with your games or whatever it is you do.”

River’s stomach churned. Mia’s little girl, Ava—her whole life was here. Her toys, her friends, the stray cat she’d adopted behind the garden wall. And now, they’d be ripped from her. All because of him.

"Please... please don’t—" His breath caught on the plea.

"What was that?" His father cupped a hand around his ear.

"I’ll do whatever you want. Just don’t do this."

His father’s eyes narrowed. "You care about this woman, huh?"

River shrugged, voice small. "Guess so."

His father’s lip stayed curled, but his tone turned almost casual. "Okay, son."

River gritted his teeth to keep his mouth shut. Here it comes…

“But Maury over here has to break your arm.”

River’s sapphire eyes grew wide. *Break his arm?*

Tears burned the corners of his eyes. He scanned his father's face, desperate for a flicker of mercy or some cruel joke. Nothing.

But his competition—he wouldn't be able to compete with a broken arm. He'd worked so hard… years of practice. It was the only sport he liked. A break would ruin the entire season.

"You took something from me, so now I'm going to take something from you," his father explained. "Maury will retrieve the watch. The police won't know a thing. But he's going to break your arm. And if you tell anyone it wasn't an accident at the gym, I'll pay your coach to lie. Then I'll make you quit for good."

Everything he loved, his father always found some way to use it against him. Twisted into leverage. Reason number one to never *love* anything.

The Maury guy loomed behind him, Ex-special ops, built like a granite cliff face.

River swallowed hard. He held out his arm, lips pressed in a tight line. Maury reached out and gripped him.

A memory surfaced as he did it. A dream.

He'd lost someone. Couldn't say who. Only that they mattered more than anything.

A large man, larger than Maury, gripped his arm, but he had to save the child.

What child? He has no real friends.

River snatched his arm away, breath hitching, clutching his skull with confusion that was ready to crack open from the inside.

Maury laughed, mistaking it for fear of him. "Poor Mia."

River shoved past his father and tore up the stairs. The tears came anyway, no matter how hard he fought them. He wiped at his face in a frantic blur. *Only babies cried.*

Do other people have dreams like that? Is there something wrong with him?

What does it all mean?

He wanted someone to tell him. For someone see him. To say he wasn't broken.

Mia did that for him, and now she was gone.

He yanked a picture frame off the shelf of his mother, smiling, holding him when he was five. Her hair was long, dark, floating like silk around both their faces.

What if he got it from her?

Did she see something, and that's why she left?

Did she see something…*in him*?

"Why didn't you take me with you?" He said out loud as if she could hear, hoping somehow, she might.

He kicked his door closed and let the tears fall, hot and bitter. *But only babies cried.*

And apparently, that's what he was. A baby. A coward. The kind of person who let good people get deported and begged for a mother who didn't want him.

Why didn't she want him?

He hurled the frame. The glass shattered, sharp and final. As if he could scare the feeling out of himself. But a cold calm settled instead.

The anger he felt… the darkness. It was her fault.

And she abandoned him—with a monster. Who does that?

She was the monster. She was as bad as him, if not worse. He won't cry for her ever again. No more crying at all.

He was alone, and that was how he would always be.

Completely alone.

Love was leverage. He wouldn't give anyone that kind of weapon against him again.

Never again.

Two weeks later, he quit his gymnastics team and never competed again.

Duncan's Journal - In the Days of Midnight Sun

Something has changed about the planet.
I have no instruments in front of me—no readings, no charts.
But I feel it.
The elders say the spirits are restless.
And lately... I'm beginning to believe them.
When you're out here—truly out here—something shifts inside you.
Your senses sharpen. You notice things you once dismissed.
The winds murmur secrets.
The ground hums with purpose.
It sounds ridiculous, especially for a man of science.
But I feel it in my bones.
And after the Great Disaster, you have to wonder...
Was that it? Or is there more?

One

River stirred from the cold air slipping through a canvas doorway, icy tendrils curling across his face and bare arm. Above him, feathers and sinew-threaded charms swayed like muted wind chimes from the fur-lined ceiling that kept out the glare of the midnight sun.

Typical. Someone couldn't even bother closing the door.

Tamar walked in. "Morning," she said, that fake, trying-to-be-nice tone laced into her voice. He rose with a low sigh, popping his neck before tying back his shoulder-length hair.

She offered him a neatly folded fur. White, soft, and clearly holding something inside. "Happy birthday."

River eyed it without reaching out. "You know I hate birthdays."

"I know." She shoved it into his lap, her expression softening. "But you're getting a gift anyway."

"I shouldn't have told you when it was."

She sighed with a weary gaze and walked off.

Clearly, she wanted him to open it, but the timing wasn't right. He wouldn't pretend to accept some loving gesture when they weren't getting along.

Tamar pulled out wooden bowls from the canvas sacks she used to keep them clean. "What would you like for breakfast?"

"I get breakfast?" Usually, when she was mad, she'd make

him fend for himself.

She shook her head. “I know you think I’m a horrible wife, but I would never let you go without breakfast on your birthday."

"I never said you were horrible."

“Well, your actions say it.”

He rolled his eyes. “No, they don’t,” he sang in a weary sigh, pushing the words out.

A dark-haired brown-eyed girl ran in through the door laughing with an older boy chasing her. She ran under the protection of Tamar, hugging her legs as the blue-eyed boy growled at her like a bear.

"Mommy, tell Heilo to stop!"

“Come on, you two, sit down.” She guided them to the soft fur rug on the gravel ground.

River stood up. "Morning Heilo." He ruffled his blonde hair. When he was born, it was feathery and black as night. At about one, it fell out and grew back blonde. Never—in his wildest dreams, did River imagine Tamar and him would have a blonde kid.

"Morning, Daddy," Heilo said as he picked at his teeth.

"Morning, Baby Girl." River bent down and kissed Bly’s dark curls. She mumbled a sweet *morning* back as he joined them, legs folded on the soft caribou rug.

They were parents, at such a young age. How do you teach children about the world when you’re still trying to figure it out yourself?

It didn’t weigh on him the same way it did Tamar. He’d accepted the consequences. Eternal abstinence wasn’t an option.

Of course, she did have it worse. Childbirth, out here, was terrifying. Every baby he risked losing her.

But every hunt, she risked losing him.

Tamar handed Bly a bowl. "After breakfast, I'll take them to Duncan's.”

"Uh-oh." Heilo nudged his sister. "That means they have to talk without us hearing."

"Never mind, you." Tamar handed him a bowl of Akutaq—artic ice cream. Berries and chilled animal fat, it was the closest thing to old world ice cream anyone could remember.

The kids shouted for joy and dug right in.

River stared at it. "There's no meat?"

Tamar tilted her head to the side. "Well, if you don't like what I made, you can always cook for yourself."

River sighed. "That's what I thought."

Tamar set her shoulders back, with a frown. "Heilo, Bly." She smiled at them. "Go eat outside with the rest of the camp."

"Yes, Mama," Heilo said as he took his sister by the hand.

She waited until the kids left, and narrowed her eyes. "You want to do this now? Really?"

He shrugged. "Do what?"

She gritted her teeth and placed a hand on her forehead. "Are you seriously going to pretend you don't know?"

He dropped his bowl and got up. "He's not hunting."

"We're not even going to talk about it? That's it? Decision made?"

How does he get her to understand? He had the dream as a kid, but it never left him. He knows the child is Heilo. The blonde hair was a dead giveaway.

"River…" She hung her head. "It was just a dream. The whole community sees the talent Heilo has. The food he could bring. You can't expect him to want to sew."

"There was a time when you had faith in my dreams."

"And sometimes they come true, but sometimes—they are just a dream."

He sat on his bed, putting his outer fur trousers on that had a hole in them at one knee. Thank goodness it was still summer. He displayed it with two hands.

She put her hands on her hips. "Oh are we going to talk about that now? Nice attempt at changing the subject."

He reached under his bed for his boots. "Maybe with Heilo sewing at least someone will handle my clothing."

She scoffed and shook her head at him. "Is that what this is really about? You're going to force your son's entire life centered around your needs? How could you be so selfish?"

"Selfish? For needing clothes that actually fit?" He stood. "You're the one who gets offended if I even mention your stitches are too tight."

Tamar let out a bitter laugh. "Says the man who can't take an ounce of criticism."

"Like anyone could survive being married to you without learning to take it," he muttered.

"Oh right." She tilted her head to the side, holding a hand to her chest. "*I'm* the critical one in this relationship."

He shoved his boots on and headed for the door.

"Where are you going?" her tone softened.

Away from this. "Hunt."

"On your birthday?"

He paused, not turning around. "It's just another day, Tamar. Grow up." He lifted the heavy fur door and left.

River tore across the taiga hills, breaths burning sharp in his lungs, legs pounding over uneven ground. The melt had shifted the earth beneath him, soft in places, jagged in others, but his legs and ankles could handle it. They moved on instinct now.

This—this was freedom.

No politics. No small talk. No fake pleasantries. Just one rule: catch the food, or go hungry.

And right now, the food was winning.

Kallik ran ahead, silent and relentless as ever. At fifty-two, the man moved like age had forgotten him. River rarely admired anyone, but he might make an exception for Kallik

Might.

He was a kind man, the way a stone was kind: quiet, steady, and unyielding—harmless until disturbed, yet formidable once provoked. He didn't say much, but when he did, you listened. Because if you didn't, the Artic would finish the sentence for you.

At the front of the Pack, Kallik slowed, eyes sweeping the terrain. The caribou had veered off. Harkin's spear likely still lodged in its flank. But the blood trail had gone dry.

Kallik tipped his head. The silence lingered longer than it should have. "Big John?"

Big John moved up, crouched low, fingers brushing the wind-crusted dirt. He pointed left. "That way."

River didn't wait. He launched forward, spear tight in hand. The others followed, packs thudding against their backs.

Harkin pulled ahead for a second, fast and reliable. Kallik always said he had a hunter's lungs. River clenched his jaw and pushed harder.

The goal wasn't to outrun the bull. It was to outlast it. To break it down, one mile at a time.

Kallik always had to remind River of that, wagging a callused finger. "Slow and steady wins the race, *Snow Rabbit*."

The caribou finally came into view. It had caught their scent. Its legs churned harder now, but the rhythm was off. River saw it in the stride, fatigue setting in.

It wasn't *if* anymore. Just *when*.

He grinned. A summer bull. Big. Full of meat and fat. If they brought it down, the camp would eat well.

Most of the Pack used arrows. They were faster, quieter, and easier to craft from whatever they could scavenge. Spears were heavier, riskier, nearly impossible to replace. But theirs were different.

Forged from scraps of the old shuttle, out of carbon struts and plating, salvaged and shaped to kill. Only the Moon Crew carried them. The Arctic Team hated them. Too clumsy, wasted energy, they said. Too old-world.

Maybe they were right. Or maybe they just didn't like weapons that reminded them of the earth burning.

Harkin surged forward, in an underhanded hurl, his aluminum spear cut clean through the air. It struck true, burying deep into the bull's back leg.

The animal groaned—a low, guttural sound—and stumbled to a halt, sides heaving.

Kallik raised a hand. "Hold."

The crew slowed, fanning into a wide semicircle. No one moved in. A cornered caribou could still kill you.

The bull stared them down. Antlers lowered. Body trembling.

Kallik gave a sharp *whoop*. A few echoed him. Not to scare the thing, but to anchor it. Keep its eyes forward. Keep it from looking for a way out.

Then, two fingers flicked.

Arrows flew.

The bull collapsed in a violent shudder, the impact rumbling the ground and lifting dust into the air. River lowered his weapon, lungs tight, heartbeat loud in his skull.

Hunger and exhaustion fought for space in his chest. He moved in with the others, every step careful. They didn't rush.

A downed caribou was even more dangerous. And panic made everything worse, for the animal, and for them.

Four hunters moved first, catching its antlers and holding steady. Not to overpower—just to hold.

Kallik stepped in next, calm as ever. Breath puffed from the animal's nostrils in short, uneven bursts. He crouched beside it, pressed a weathered hand to its thick neck, and met its eye.

"Thank you, brother," he said, voice low and steady.

He drew his blade, a carved stone edge lashed to a bone handle with sinew, and slid it beneath the caribou's neck.

One clean pull.

Blood spilled over the gravel, soaking into the cold earth. The animal shuddered.

Kallik stayed with it, stroking the fur along its shoulder, murmuring quiet sounds and singing until the body relaxed.

Its eyes dulled. The pain left.

"Go in peace," he whispered. "Return to the land."

To look an animal in the eye before taking its life—that was the purest way to eat.

Back in the old world, River would walk into grocery stores, grabbed steak from a freezer without blinking. He had no idea what he was missing.

If you couldn't look a creature in the eye and understand the life you were taking, you didn't deserve to eat it.

Kallik tucked the blade into his belt and barked instructions. River and Big John tied ropes around the antlers, ready to drag the carcass back on thick canvas.

River smirked. Big John's knots were tighter, neater. Probably muscle memory from all those yeehaw rodeo years. River hated being second-best at anything, but Big John made it hard to mind.

"It's a big bull," Big John said, impressed.

Kallik nodded. "Should feed the whole community well. Nice job, boys."

Six men on the rope at a time, swapping out as they dragged the beast home across canvas tarps, Kallik leading the way.

After many miles, they reached a fresh pool of water. The pack leader raised a fist, and the group halted.

He stepped forward, crouched, and dipped his fingers into the pool. "This the one you were talking about?"

River gave a slow nod and blink in confirmation.

Kallik tapped the side of his cheek. "Yeah, it's nice. An extra warm summer has its gifts." Due to the warmer weather that year, the elders had taken them lower south than normal.

"Is it safe, though?" Big John asked. "Shouldn't we get this meat back home?"

Kallik scanned the horizon. "I don't see any close. What do you think?" He glanced again at River.

"We'll keep an eye out."

Kallik rose, squaring his shoulders with a clap. "All right boys! Bath time."

Groans erupted. "But it's cold!" someone whined.

Kallik planted his hands on his hips. "No complaining. If I bring you back smelling like this, the women might not let us back in."

The men laughed, but Kallik wasn't entirely joking. They all smelled awful. River could barely stand being within three feet of any of them.

Kallik shrugged off his parka, revealing a round, soft, old-man belly. "Last three in drags the beast home," he called.

"Only three?" Carson wailed.

Next to him, Kodiak looked crushed. His high ponytail swayed in the light breeze. "Man, that's harsh."

River stabbed his spear into the dirt and untied his belt. He kicked off his hide boots and rolled up the cuff of his pants, revealing a handgun strapped to his calf.

"What's the matter?" he said, grinning at Kodiak. "Too much for you?" He unhooked the holster and tossed it onto the pile of gear. Then stripped down to a pair of bright blue gym shorts, the last relic of a life long gone.

The sun beat warm on his back. The wind was cold. It felt good.

An actual bath—yeah, that would be nice. It was too far from home to come out this way alone. Too dangerous.

River took off running and launched off the cliff in a forward flip, legs kicking the whole way down, and crashing into the cold water below.

The men whooped and hollered as he surfaced, snapping his head back to fling the hair from his eyes.

"How's the water?" Harkin shouted.

River grinned mid-backstroke. "It's horrible," he called, shaking his head. "Stay out."

Which, of course, meant *everyone* jumped in.

River rolled his eyes while a line of hunters followed each other like kids at recess, diving into the deep with hollers and war cries. Water churned. Splashing. Kicking. Shoving.

It was one of the most refreshing things River had felt in a long time. Even with the chill, getting all that filth scrubbed off your skin felt like a full reset. Rare. Clean. Alive.

Big John stepped to the edge. The men scattered and yelped. He gave them a long, mischievous look—

And cannonballed in. A wall of water exploded outward, crashing against the rocks and echoing off the cliffs.

Noah was the last in. He lingered at the ledge.

"Come on, Goldilocks!" Harkin yelled.

"Is the princess scared?" Kodiak added.

Eventually, he jumped. Which was more like a fall. He bobbed up whining. "Shouldn't've bothered getting in, since I have to drag it home anyway."

"You need the cardio," Carson said, slapping him on the shoulder hard enough to leave a red mark.

Kodiak ruffled Noah's hair like an older cousin with no sense of boundaries. "Yeah, you're looking fluffier than usual."

Noah shoved him off, unfettered.

Zack—Carson's old teammate from Lunar Team Three—floated on his back, arms stretched behind his head. "It's not so cold once you get used to it."

"Whatever man, it's freezing," Carson muttered, dunking under and splashing water up into Zack's face.

One by one, they climbed out of the water, shaking off like a pet after a bath and dressing once the chill air dried their skin.

Carson emerged like a wet cat, teeth chattering. "Big John. Fire. Now."

Big John raised an eyebrow at Kallik, who shrugged. "It's your fire bundle."

"Yeah, but I make those for emergencies."

"It's an emergency!" Carson screeched.

River watched, unsympathetic, as Big John pulled a fire bundle from his bag. Shrub willow, soft tundra wood, dried grass, and moss, all woven into compact pallets and slicked with seal blubber.

What a waste.

Light and easy to haul, Big John's bundles were genius. He'd figured out how to merge old-world survival skills with Arctic resources. Made them for the whole camp. Even the Arctic people used them now.

He struck flint to the bundle and it caught. The men crowded in tight around the flame, hunching low in a circle, squeezing Carson out.

"Hey!" Carson shoved Kodiak. "Move it, I'm freezing."

"There's not enough room," Kodiak said, shaking his head.

"Make some, man." Carson tried to wedge himself between Kodiak and Takumi.

"Dude." Takumi raised his hands, flashing that annoyingly perfect grin. "Blame Mr. Clean over there. He's the one who convinced Kallik to mandate bath time because of your smell." He shot a glare at River.

River didn't blink. Just held the stare. Filed it away for later.

"You can't blame that all on me," Carson said. "I know what you ate last night." He clamped a hand over his nose. "Never thought I'd miss the methane tanks."

"There's still room next to Upa," Kodiak offered, pointing to the large man hogging a whole side of the circle.

Upa scratched himself, a cloud of Arctic mosquitoes circling his shoulders. He let loose a bridge troll belch and rubbed his swollen belly.

Carson recoiled. "Yeah, and there's a reason that real estate's still available."

The men turned their backs, ignoring him.

“Did you see the massive nuts on that bull?” Kodiak asked Takumi.

Takumi raised an eyebrow. “How could you *not*?”

Carson pressed his lips together, arms crossed, rubbing them for warmth. “The fire was my idea!”

Nobody answered.

Carson glanced around, grinning like someone about to commit a crime. He popped his thumb into his mouth—sloooowly pulled it out—then jammed it straight into Dex’s ear.

“WHAT THE—” Dex roared, grabbing Carson by the back of his parka and flipping him over his shoulder, his boots kissing the fire. “Carson, you freak! I don’t want your nasty spit in my ear.”

Kodiak and Takumi cracked up.

“Goodness knows where that mouth has been,” Takumi added.

“You don’t want to know,” Kodiak said through his teeth. He cupped his hands as if he were a town crier: “From henceforth, Dex shall be known… as Wet Willy!”

Zack shook his head. “Jeez, you're a dork.”

“No!” Dex wiped furiously at his ear, digging with his pinky. “I’m not.” He stormed back toward the water. “I’m not!”

Harkin chuckled, peering back. “You missed by about two inches, man.” He held up the measurement with his fingers.

Kodiak half-smiled. “Then it would’ve been Barbecue Carson.”

“I wouldn’t even eat that.” Takumi wrinkling his nose. Laughter rippled through the group.

“At least we wouldn’t have to hear his yammering anymore,” Harkin muttered, rubbing one eye.

Carson brushed grass off himself and plopped into Dex’s spot, hands spread to the fire with a smirk. He took a deep breath of fresh air—

And yelped like a burly man getting hit with a surprise ice

enema. Dex had shoved a handful of frozen rocks into his hide pants.

Carson twisted and flailed, fishing pebbles from places they should never be.

The group roared with laughter.

Carson yanked down his pants and mooned them all, backing his bare backside up to the fire, disgustingly lit up.

"No one wants to see that," Takumi gagged. "Put the polar cheeks away."

The others gagged and groaned, pelting him with gravel and dirt, laughing too hard to aim straight.

River stood off to the side, arms crossed, Big John beside him, both out of the firelight.

"Want to warm up?" Kallik asked. "I can make them move."

"I'm fine," River said. He'd rather freeze than wedge in beside—*them*.

"Sometimes I feel like I'm back in middle school," Big John chuckled.

Kallik shrugged. "They need to get their funnies out. Now's a good time."

Funnies? River snorted to himself. He wouldn't call it *funnies*. He'd call it a severe case of moron.

Right on cue, Upa launched to his feet, planted himself like a siege weapon, and spread his butt cheeks and expelled what could only be described as a pressurized nightmare, directly at Carson's face. Carson squealed and flailed backward, boots scraping as the men howled with laughter.

"Dude, you wasted it!" Kodiak scolded. "You should've done it in the fire—would've made it warmer."

"That won't work," Harkin muttered.

Kodiak stood tall over him. "You wanna bet?"

River sighed, rubbing his face. It was like tolerating an entire team of Ringos. What could possibly be worse?

Zack and Kodiak braced Upa, pointing his rear toward the

fire.

"Okay… Ready. Set. Go!" Kodiak commanded, slapping his back.

"I can't do it on command," Upa squealed.

"Then you're *useless*," Kodiak declared in a frustrated high-pitch squeak. "What good are you if you can't fart in the fire?"

Big John let out the laugh he'd clearly been trying to hold in. "Forget middle school. It's like an old-world frat house."

"It's the hunting team," River added. "We *are* the frat house of the old world."

Kallik chuckled and laid a hand on River's shoulder. "Guess that makes me the Dean." He raised his voice. "All right, boys! Put out the fire and prep to move."

The men scattered, and followed orders. River jogged to his gear by the waterline, just below the slope. Behind him, Harkin stooped over the meat, looping rope around one hand.

"You were one of the last three?" River asked, strapping his hoister back on.

Harkin grinned. "I know, right? I've never liked cold water, always the last one in at the pool. Before, you know…"

Pools. That word hung in the air. Even before the quakes cracked the planet open, swimming pools had become a luxury. A relic.

All it took was one horrifying incident: a quake split a pool in two, dragging five children into the earth. No one trusted them after that.

River nodded once, eyes scanning the slope.

Harkin hefted the rope over his shoulder. "But I'm sure you had, what—twenty of them?"

"Not quite," River muttered with a dry scoff.

A flick of movement. Too big. Too white.

Bear.

It crested the ridge, silent and sudden. Massive shoulders loomed, blotting out the last of their laughter. Rippled white fur. Demon eyes. The worst intentions.

River flinched back. “Harkin, run!”

The bear lunged. Its jaws locked on Harkin’s leg.

He screamed. A tearing, raw sound that didn’t sound human.

River dove for the nearest spear and hurled it at the bear. It missed, clattering uselessly across the rock.

No.

Arrows flew from the ridge above. The bear dragged Harkin backward toward the water, each paw kicking up gravel and leaving behind a dark blood trail.

Kallik charged in with a roar, both hands locked around his knife. He slammed it into the bear’s side.

The bear’s teeth dropped Harkin.

It whirled around and sunk its jaw into Kallik’s arm.

Kallik braced, teeth bared, straining to pry the jaws apart. River dove in, rolled beside him, and yanked the pistol from his holster. The bear turned on him, mouth opening wide.

River fired.

The bullet punched through the bear’s open maw, straight into the skull. Weight of the large beast fell on him. River went down, bear fur suffocating his face, the heat of it still alive. He grunted, struggling to breath, shoving at the bulk. It didn’t budge.

With a heave, he scooted free from under the dead mound. Kodiak and Nukilik were already at Harkin’s side, trying to hold him still. Blood soaked the ground.

Harkin writhed, howling through clenched teeth. Kodiak tied a tourniquet from canvas strips and braced it with a stick, tightening it down until the bleeding stopped. Takumi was with Kallik, wrapping his arm in seal-cloth bindings.

Big John kicked the bear’s side, surveying it. “Man-hunter. Based on the tracks, he was stalking us.”

“Must’ve thought he could snatch Harkin while he was alone,” Dex said beside them, exhaling hard.

Takumi looked up from his bandaging, eyes sharp. "Someone had the genius idea to let our guard down in the middle of nowhere."

River's chest clenched. His eyes softened. Was this his fault?

He glanced at Harkin, pale, shaking, and going into shock.

River winced. His eyes dropped to his gun. The same gun he used to shoot—

Driscal's serene face. Eyes shut. The moment all the air left his body.

Big John's hand landed on his shoulder, grounding him. River sucked the thought back down, popped the magazine, and checked it like that had been his plan all along. "Down to two bullets."

"Bears are hard to kill," Big John murmured. "A 9mm won't do it unless you're practically up its nose. You got there as fast as you could."

River picked up his fallen spear. "I hate spears."

"Well, you better start loving 'em," Big John said. "'Cause once that ammo's gone, those and arrows are all you've got."

River crouched beside Kallik, resting a hand on his arm. Kallik shoved Takumi out of the way and grabbed the front of River's parka, dragging him close.

His eyes were bloodshot, feral with pain. "Get them home," he rasped.

River nodded, steady.

Big John bent and hauled Harkin up over his shoulders. Harkin screamed, shaking from the effort.

"I've got you, man," Big John said.

They tied the polar bear for dragging. Carson, Dex, Zack, Kodiak, Takumi, and Nukilik took that load. Two kills on one trip. But the second wasn't worth it.

River walked back to the bull, grabbed the rope Harkin had dropped, and slung it over his shoulder. He glanced at Upa and Noah. "Ready?"

Noah gave a solemn nod.
Together, they dragged the beast home.

Duncan's Journal Entry - Days of Midnight Sun

Bears are the masters now.
They watch us from a distance—
acknowledging some unspoken truce.
"You stay out of our territory, and we will allow you to live in yours."
Funny. It used to be the other way around.
They know this world belongs to them again.
And we're the new endangered species.
Where we hunt, where we travel, how we move,
all dictated by the bears.
No one goes head-to-head with one and walks out unscathed.
One man alone? Not a chance.
Four might bring one down.
But someone always comes back broken.
That's why I never leave the village.
Some would call it cowardice.
But what would I be risking my life for?
The elders never questioned it.
When we joined this community, we swore to follow their guidance.
I've honored that vow. I stay where I'm told.
And yet... I feel guilty.
Is there room left in this world for scholars?
Or am I the true endangered species?

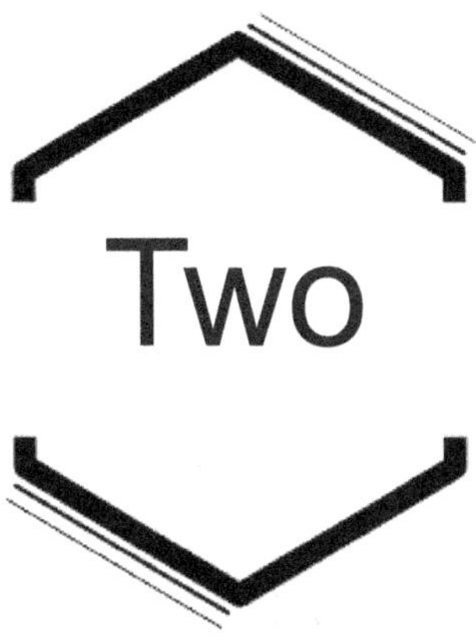

Two

WITH A STONE knife, Tamar scraped tiny, prickly hairs off a caribou hide stretched across a stick frame in the open air, envisioning a new pair of pants.

The pants River demanded.

The other seamstresses—though most called them *sewers*—sat in a loose circle, each hunched over their own half-finished garments.

Sewing. Always sewing.

Tamar didn't grow things anymore.

She sewed. An activity she never knew she hated until it became her profession.

Arnaq—the little show-off—was already done with her work for the day. Her hair up in a dark twist, she pointed a stem of wild celery she was chewing at Tamar. "Let me get this straight. The guy made it *crystal clear* he didn't want to celebrate his birthday, and you pushed it on him, anyway?"

Tamar sighed, hands falling into her lap. "He did so much for mine. It felt wrong not to return the favor."

Arnaq cocked her head to the side, eyes wide with mock sympathy. "So this is about *you*?"

Tamar tossed a hand in her direction. "Since when are you on his side?"

"Oh, I'm not. I can't stand River. I hope a polar bear eats

his head off."

"And yet, I still talk to you."

"That's because I'm the only sensible person in this entire camp." She leaned in. "That—and you're using me for my sewing skills."

Tamar returned the lean in, smirking. "Arnaq, you are my only hope."

"I'm not sure there is any hope for you. Maybe you should join your husband on the hunting team."

"You kidding?" Tamar shook her head. "At least this way I get a break from him every time he leaves."

A ripple of laughter spread through the circle.

"We get a break from *them all*," Arnaq corrected. "Never thought I'd miss working in daycare. At least then you had cute little kids to hold. Instead, we are stuck with a circus of stinky hairy men who can't even patch their own butts."

The sun finally broke through the clouds, treating Tamar's skin to some much-needed sunlight. It gleamed off the lagoon near the village, casting silver across the water.

The other sewers had the same idea. All the women, plus two men, sat together in the center of the village, soaking in the nicer-than-normal day.

Three weeks of cloud cover, and they'd finally gotten a break. The need for sunlight felt like a kind of hunger. Your body craved it, remembering something you hadn't had in a long time—and wanted back.

Badly.

The plants fed off the sun. The animals ate the plants. And people ate the animals.

Humans were made to need its rays, were drawn to it, but at the same time, its radiation aged you. Burned you.

Because that's the thing, isn't it?

The very thing that gives you life… will eventually kill you.

Tamar took her knife and cut down along the hide.

Arnaq shook her head. "You're still not leaving enough slack for the seams."

"I thought we were trying to save as much skin as possible."

"*I* could sew seams that short," Arnaq said, celery stem bouncing in her mouth. "But you? No, no, Boo Boo. Don't mimic me that close." She barely smacked the top of Tamar's head with the celery.

"Well, great. Now what am I going to do? I just wasted another hide."

"And your hunter still has no pants."

Tamar narrowed her eyes. She didn't mention they were in the middle of a fight over pants. "Someone's been eavesdropping."

"You two argued for three days before the hunt. *Everyone* eavesdropped," Arnaq said, watching two women pass with waterskins.

"Privacy doesn't exist here," Kaya, Harkin's wife, chimed. "Not really."

She wasn't wrong.

Every embarrassing moment, every awkward groan, every intimate night with a spouse—seen, heard, and absorbed by the whole camp. It was one part of ancient life Tamar still couldn't get used to. Maybe never would.

There were no pretenses anymore. No keeping up appearances. Everyone around you knew exactly how gross, irritable, or petty you could be.

In that sense, River—with his constant attitude—didn't seem so out of place anymore.

And yet… there was something freeing in it. No more smiling for strangers. No more small talk with coworkers that bored you. No more keeping up the act.

The game had changed. And the new objective was survival.

Sura, Osha's twenty-two-year-old daughter and her spitting

image, sprang up, pointing at Tamar's stitching and shaking her head. No words. Just the judgment.

Kaya paused her stitching and glanced at the uneven hide stretched in front of Tamar.

"Is he going to be expecting new pants once he gets back?" Her lips pressed together, eyes soft with worry.

Tamar sighed, heat rising to her cheeks. "He's too demanding."

"He can't wear pants that are too small for him," Arnaq cut in.

Tamar raised an eyebrow, lips tight.

"Oh for goodness sakes." Arnaq flung a hand out. "Wearing pants that fit won't stop a polar bear from biting his head off."

"That's true," Tamar muttered, eyeing the botched piece. Fourth attempt. But she wasn't about to let anyone know how many hides she'd wasted.

Kaya reached over and rubbed her arm. "You'll get the hang of it. Don't be so hard on yourself."

"Tell you what," Arnaq offered. "I need a new pair for Tuila. I can use the pair you botched and I'll trade you a fresh skin. Finish what you're working on now for Heilo."

Tuila—Arnaq and Takumi's little girl was always outgrowing something.

"Thank you," Tamar murmured, remembering River's words weeks ago. The community couldn't keep fronting skins for her. Couldn't keep covering her mistakes.

She had no choice but to figure this out, and fast.

She finished cutting the hide, smaller this time. Heilo needed new pants anyway. That kid burned through them like a seal through fish. He probably already had a hole in the last pair she made him.

Tamar bit her bottom lip and kept cutting. Fast, frustrated.

Arnaq grabbed her wrist. "Slow down."

"But now I have two pairs to make."

"Go get a new skin. I'll cut this one." She grinned. "Patience, grasshopper. You'll get it."

Tamar shook her head. It hadn't taken the rest of the Moon Crew this long.

Across the circle, Jason held up a new parka while Osha praised his stitching. Even Oliver was doing better than her. They made it look easy.

She'd never struggled like this before.

There were two jobs in the community: hunters and sewers. Nothing else.

It wasn't gendered. It wasn't ranked.

It was just survival.

Hunters kept them fed. Sewers kept them warm.

Both mattered. But she was failing at hers.

Whoops and howls echoed in the distance. The hunting team was back. "About time," said Kaya.

Arnaq nodded. Tamar and her cup their hands to copy the sounds with the rest of the clothes-makers. Whoops and hollers echoed throughout the village. The three elders came out of their tents and headed to greet the hunting team.

The sewers all left their skins and pulled their knives out of their belts, heading for the processing circle. Tamar tied her long hair back.

Time to get messy.

They halted at the sight of Harkin and Kallik being hobbled home. The wounds said enough.

Another bear.

Kaya fell to the ground, hand clamped over her mouth. Arnaq knelt beside her, wrapping an arm around her shoulders. "Get them to Natasha," she yelled. "Now."

Big John shifted Harkin on his back. "We're all going to hear it from her," he muttered.

The Moon crew called her Laney. But to Kallik, she was Wife.

Behind them, the rest of the hunters dropped to their knees

around the bull. Heads bowed, voices low. They sang. Not joyfully, not loud, but with a solemnity so old it seemed to move the world itself. A song of sorrow, for a life that ended so theirs could go on.

The deeper the grief, the deeper the thanks, the more meat they'd be blessed with. At least, that's what the elders said.

Tamar didn't stop to join them. She walked beside Big John, her hand resting on Harkin's leg where it hung looped over his arm. Heat bled through his skin.

Up close, it was worse. Blood soaked his clothes. His lips were pale. His eyes barely tracked.

Tamar's stomach twisted. This was the only way she still worked with her first love now—when someone was sick or dying.

She handed over Rhododendron groenlandicum—Bay Tea she'd prepared earlier that day. It wouldn't be enough.

Harkin's wounds were deep. Bay Tea was only a mild antiseptic.

They eased Harkin onto a padded pallet inside Natasha's tent. Kallik was already there, jaw clenched, blood already soaking the bandage Laney had wrapped around his arm.

"Why were there no sentries on duty?" she snapped.

"I know, I know. I messed up." Kallik waved a hand.

"There's no room for mistakes out here," she growled. "You of all people should know that."

Her eyes fell on Harkin. "*Heavens almighty.*" Natasha breathed as she hurried to his side. One hand brushed his cheek. The other hovered over his swollen, purpling leg. "Oh, Harkin, my poor boy."

She placed two fingers just beneath his jaw, on the side of his neck.

"Is he… dead?" Arnaq asked, barely above a whisper.

Natasha shook her head. "No. He's in shock."

Kaya was curled off to the side, rocking, soft whimpers lifting with each breath. Tamar pulled her close, one arm around her shoulders, Kaya's head pressed to her chest.

Laney examined the tourniquet. "How long has this been on him?"

"About three hours," Big John answered.

"Gather rocks to elevate his leg."

Big John nodded and moved fast.

"Still no Usnea?" Laney asked, eyes square on Tamar.

She shook her head. "Not since the warm snap."

Laney looked at her, tight-lipped, but said nothing, leaving a pinch of guilt in Tamar's stomach.

It hadn't been cold enough. Usnea liked wet, cool tree bark. She'd searched already. The treeline was seven miles out. Years ago, she found some deeper in.

But that was through wolf territory.

Ever since River's last encounter with them, she was scared to go back.

"Okay." Natasha stood, straightening her shoulders. "We have a decision to make."

Kaya began to cry, shaking her head as if she could deny the moment from happening.

"There's no way to save the leg?" Kallik asked, his voice thick.

"I can try," Natasha answered. "But I think it will be fruitless. The bear bit clean through the muscle. Even if I cauterize it, there's likely bacteria deep inside. Tamar's herb mixture may help, but I doubt it'll reach far enough. Once gangrene sets in…"

"If we try," Kallik asked. "How long until we know?"

"Once he goes septic," she said, shaking her head. "And that's hard to stop, even with pre-Disaster medicine."

Kallik pressed a hand to his forehead. "So we either take the leg and save his life, or risk keeping it and losing him."

"It's a horrible choice," Laney said.

Tamar stepped forward. "If I get the Usnea—"

"The tincture will take at least twenty-four hours to make,"

Natasha interrupted. "And that's *if* you had it with you now. We don't have it, so it's best to remove the infected flesh."

"You don't understand my husband," Kaya said, voice tight with grief. "If you take his leg, he'd rather die. What kind of life is that? Having to depend on everyone just to move?"

"We'll make him a crutch," Natasha said.

"And he won't hunt anymore," Kaya countered. "Being useful is the most important thing to him."

"He could sew," Natasha offered. "Sewers are just as valuable. There's no shame in it."

"While our people deeply believe that, my husband still has too much of the old world in him. That will give him a deep depression."

"He's one of the best hunters," Arnaq interrupted. "We barely made it through last winter as it is. What are we going to do, being down one of our best? And he is still a mouth to feed."

"Arnaq?" Tamar scolded.

Arnaq crossed her arms. "It's true. Don't act like I'm cruel for saying what everyone is thinking. We no longer have the luxury of catering to emotions over facts."

Natasha turned to her husband. "That's why *you* need to be part of this conversation. Winter is on its way. And as important as Harkin is to us—"

"I cannot make this decision."

"But you're Pack leader—"

"I will not!" he roared, slamming a fist into his thigh.

The entire tent went still. No one moved. No one breathed.

Kallik's anger was rare. Tamar had only seen it once before. Back when the Moon Crew and Artic Team first joined and tensions were high. He was furious then, demanding the two groups unify.

Kaya watching with wide eyes and broke in tears, covering her face with her hands. Tamar continued to hold her close, rubbing her arm with her lose hand.

Kallik sighed and his shoulders fell. He studied Harkin with eyes that seemed to deeply wish things had turned out different. “Kaya will choose. She is the one most affected. She will choose.”

“Keep the leg,” she whimpered. “Do what you can to save him.”

Natasha nodded and got to work.

Duncan's Journal - Days of Midnight Sun

The Elders.
Three of them.
Two men and one woman—old, wise, and hardened by life.
Muktuk, Derrick, and the oldest, Ahnah, with the eyes of frozen water.
I'm told, originally, her name was Christine.
She took on her great-grandmother's name after the Disaster.
All three were raised in the world before.
All three have done their best to remember the old ways. Most of it passed down by their grandparents, cobbled together from fading memories and half-preserved traditions.
Passing knowledge on to the young, it matters more than anything now.
The Old World lost this.
We weren't interested in our elders.
We had the internet to teach us things.
But who actually used it for knowledge?
The greatest collection of human thought ever assembled, and we used it for cat videos and celebrity meltdowns.
We squandered it.
If not for Kallik, we'd be in real trouble.

His grandfather made him learn the old
ways while there was still time.
And thank the stars for that.
So much had been erased by progress.
Kallik doesn't just remember. He restores.
The Elder Circle is where he belongs.

Three

Blood steamed off the fresh kill as Tamar slid into the processing circle, blade in hand but heart off-kilter. River sat across from her, elbows deep in the bull. He looked up and their eyes locked and held.

Goosebumps rippled over her arms, and her breath hitched. Even mean—he could still take her breath away.

She didn't let it show. They just held eye contact. It had been five days since he left.

Your move, husband.

He said nothing, and refocused on his work, cutting along the leg, skinning with precision. Tamar followed suit, working her knife around the neck.

Children sat around the edge of the circle, calm and quiet, Heilo and Bly with them. No one had to holler at them to come and learn. They just did. They watched because they were supposed to. Someday, they'd need to know how to do this to survive.

Skins were too valuable to waste, meat too precious to risk. First, they watched. Later, they would do.

Tamar sighed. However, if she was being honest with herself, that was where she really belonged—in the children's circle. She worked her blade carefully around the bull's head, peeling the hide back from the skull and ears, revealing the deep red beneath.

River could do the gutting. She slit three intestines before she decided: that area was not for her. Luckily, Arnaq was there to make sure the meat hadn't been ruined, green bile painting the yellowed tundra grass underneath it.

She got some sharp looks after that. And she deserved them, but it still made her feel horrible.

To waste, was a terrible crime.

You had to have great respect for the animal. Handle it with care and precision.

It was the way.

Across the circle, Arnaq had joined the team breaking down the bear. Blood soaked the grass beneath it. Everything would be divided equally. No one went without.

If one starved, the whole camp starved.

Tamar could feel River's eyes peeking out at her, glancing over at her every once in a while. Yeah—yeah. She missed him too.

"What happened?" she asked him, almost done with the bull's neck. Her knife was no longer cutting the flesh easily. She would have to sharpen it before continuing.

"Bear attack. What does it look like?"

She rolled her eyes and shook her head. He was *so* ridiculous. How did he not realize this was an attempt at conversation. She rubbed her itchy nose with the clean part of her sleeve, biting back the irritation. "I noticed it has bullet holes in its brain."

He gave a small nod. "Down to two."

"You're the last one with a functioning gun. What are we going to do when that runs out?"

He shrugged. "People survived out here for centuries before guns."

"But we've already lost four hunters this year, not including the two now injured."

"I'll figure it out, okay?" He whistled to Zack and Carson.

"There's enough people on the bear, quit chatting and come help get this caribou done."

The two men cross over, knives ready. She raised an eyebrow at River. "Why are you giving orders? Or is that just the only thing you're good at?"

Carson slung a bloody arm around River's shoulders. "River here is now the de facto Pack leader."

River bumped him, upper lip curled.

Tamar blinked. "*Oh*, Takumi is not going to like that."

She glanced toward him. Sure enough, he stood with Nukilik, Dex, and Upa, their attention fixed on River across the field as they worked the polar bear.

River followed her gaze. "Why do you care what he thinks?"

Her lip curled. "I didn't say I did."

River yanked the skin free from the bull's leg. "It's just until Kallik gets better."

"*If* he gets better," Carson added.

River shook his head. "Harkin is in worse shape. Your concern should be with him."

Takumi's group passed them, kicking rocks in River's direction as they walked by.

River didn't flinch. Just smirked, eyes that said: *try that again.*

Takumi dipped his head at Tamar with a bright smile. "Good to see you."

Now that the chest-pounding match between those two was over, Tamar pulled out her secondary knife from her belt and got back to work in silence. Things between him and Takumi had been tense for years.

But now?

Now River was in charge. And that was going to make things between them worse.

A fur-consumed Jason plopped down next to Tamar, crossing his legs."I've been talking with Oliver after our trip, and we were thinking next time you could collect some seeds for us, so we can try a greenhouse closer to the village."

Tamar nodded. "Great idea. But good luck prying that plastic sheet from Oliver's goblin hoard," she said, wagging a finger.

Oliver had won it from her in a betting game called Bones a year ago and he'd done *nothing* with it. Valuable plastic didn't exist anymore, and it was just sitting there, in his absurd stash, collecting mold.

"I was wondering where that went!" Jason bolted upright and took off, muttering something about confiscation.

River kept cutting. His eyes narrowed and his lips pressed. "Trip?" He didn't look up. Just kept cutting in sharp slices, like the meat had personally offended him.

Tamar's chest tightened. *Here it comes*. "Yeah, they thought they might have found a set of hops down at the edge of the tree line right after you left. Wanted me to confirm it."

"Say what?"

"Hops. It's a flowering plant—Humulus lupulus."

River gave her that look. The irritated, fine-whatever one he always pulled when she used Latin.

"It's just a plant," she added, trying to humor him.

"Why didn't you just say that."

"Because there are many different plants, with different names."

They both stood, lifting the meat and fur for hauling back to their tent.

She could feel friction radiating off him, tight and silent. Maybe explaining would help?

"I honestly couldn't believe it, but when I got there, sure enough. It was nugget hops. A warm summer has many gifts," she said, smiling at him.

He didn't smile back. "You left the village without me again," he said eventually, eyes averted, jaw tight.

"Well, that's kind of a big deal. The first batch should be

almost done and then we'll know if we can use them." She continued, hoping to soften his mood.

"Use them?"

Tamar, a step ahead of him, looked over her shoulder. "Yeah. They're making a still. You know—for moonshine." She grinned.

River sighed. "Glad someone's thinking of the important things around here."

Tamar laughed but he didn't respond in any way to her joy. "Alcohol actually is a good antiseptic," she added. "We can make tinctures now. It's going to be really helpful, especially now." *With Harkin's situation.*

"True."

Tamar slowed her steps. The best time to bring it up would probably be now. "Harkin needs Usnea."

He sighed. "A plant?"

"Yeah, it's best for serious infection…in wolf territory."

He instantly shook his head in quick, furious motions. "No, absolutely not."

"But he could die!"

His eyes flashed. "We could die—" He shoved back his sleeve, revealing the long scar down his forearm.

Tamar looked away. She didn't need a reminder of the wound from the wolf attack that almost took his life. "But it's Harkin…" she said quietly, then took a step and squeezed his arm in a desperate attempt to get him to understand. "River—it's Harkin."

Three times he'd carried River home. Three times he'd saved River's life.

"There's no certainty that it would work." His eyes softened. "Are they taking his leg?"

"No, Kaya doesn't want them too."

"His leg was black. I got him home as fast as I could, but it was still bad. What did Laney say?"

"She doesn't think she can do anything without taking the

leg."

"If they take the leg," he said, barely meeting her eyes, "I'll think about it."

He got quiet again and the conversation was slipping away. She searched for something else to say—something safe, something—happier. He thought she was too critical, so… she'd try not to be. "Heilo caught five rabbits while you were gone."

"He's hunting?" he gruffed.

"Yeah, just around the camp. That should be safe enough for you." Guess that wasn't the best topic.

They passed by Arnaq, crossing her arms at River, staring him down.

Tamar gave her a nod. "And Arnaq sends her love."

He snickered. "Which body part of mine is she hoping gets eaten this time?"

"You're head, actually."

"At least it's no longer my manhood."

"And that's better than your head?"

"Well, yeah. 'Cause then I'd cease to exist."

Tamar shook her head with a grin. "You're ridiculous."

That earned a brief smile. Just as quickly, it faded. The cold returned, not in his words, but in the way he moved, the way his presence seemed to dim around her. As if some quiet part of himself was shutdown to her.

She turned to him, eyes soft and questioning. He stopped him in his tracks, but avoided her glance, looking off into the distance. She threw the fur pile in her arms down on the ground.

His eyes grew wide and he leaned away from her. "What the hell?"

"*The hell* is right." Everyone around them looked their way.

She held her arm out. "What's been up with you lately? Even before the trip. You haven't been this indifferent to me since before we got together on the moon."

His jaw locked tight, and his eyes flicked to the growing circle of attention. "You're making a scene."

She didn't care. Her stare stayed fixed and unwavering. "It's wrong to be mad at someone without telling them why."

"I'm not mad."

Tamar scoffed. "Could have fooled me."

The thing about River was that he didn't like being backed into a corner. When she fished for a compliment or a sign of affection, it usually backfired. He wasn't the guy who said what you wanted to hear. That mystery had drawn her in once. Still did, sometimes.

But it came with a cost. And right now, she was tired of paying it.

"Let's just get the meat and fur up," he muttered, walking past her to their home.

She bent down, picked up the fur bundle, and followed him inside. She set it down in the corner, out of the way. "River… talk to me."

He turned around to face her as she stepped in close, taking his hand. There was pain in his eyes, undeniable. Sharp, quiet pain.

What was going on with him?

Had something else happened out there? Was it Harkin?

Had he done something he regretted? It wasn't like him to hold things in.

Not to her.

He let her hold his hand, but his grip stayed loose as his gaze drifted away.

"Are my pants done?" he asked, low and gruff.

She blinked. "Is this all about *pants?*"

"Never said that."

"Then what?"

His mouth moved to the side, and he sighed. "You can't leave the village without me, even when you're mad at me."

Tears prickled at the edges of her eyes. Was that it? What this coldness had been about?

That couldn't be the reason. But if this was the conversation he wanted—then they'd have it.

"There's not a lot to do around here," she said softly. "At least… not things I *want* to do. I feel like I have no life other than being a mother and a wife."

"That *is* your life now." His expression tightened, arms spread. "We're supposed to be your life now."

"I didn't mean it that way," she said with a light shake of her head. "You know you and the kids are everything to me. But I need to work with plants. I can barely do that here—not like I used to. This project… it was a way to feel like myself again."

He dropped his chin, arms folding across his chest. He didn't look convinced.

"I just..." She cradled her hands to her heart. "I feel like I've lost a part of myself." She fell into him, burying her face in his chest, trying not to cry.

She wanted him to understand.

She *needed* him to understand.

After a long pause, he sighed, and wrapped his arms around her, resting his chin on her head.

"We all have."

Duncan's Journal - Days of Lingering Light

I used to miss the privacy of the old world.

Having an entire space to yourself. To do whatever you wanted, indulge in whatever desires struck, without risking your reputation. Sometimes, I just wanted to sit around in my underwear and enjoy my wife—without the voyeurism of others. But eventually, I came to understand what privacy stole from us.

Shame.

Shame and guilt are what keep the degenerate at bay. Out here, no one beats their wife or neglects their child without the whole camp knowing. You can't hide behind walls or city noise.

Everyone sees. Everyone hears.

And because of that—everyone behaves.

Individualism, consumerism, anonymity—these feed the worst in us. But community, sustainability, reputation? They demand more. They make you better.

How can you lie, steal, murder, cheat—when every eye is watching?

People used to call tribalism backwards. Primitive.

But now I see it clearly.
Tribalism gives us what we most need,
community.
It has one caveat, though.
Being the physically stronger gender, it's
on the men to safeguard the freedoms of the
women. Because history has shown—if men
unite in their demands, in their
entitlement—the result isn't strength.
It's enslavement.
As I watch the testosterone-fueled gang
that is the hunting crew,
I can't help but wonder…
What's stopping them?

Four

TAMAR BLEW OUT the qulliq, the moon-shaped oil lamp Osha had taught her to carve and tend. A crack split its thin wall, born from the thermal shock the first time she'd tried to light it.

It was a huge disappointment. The lamp had taken over a week to make, grinding stone to stone.

But she wouldn't make a new one. Not until she could carry the weight of this life—the marriage, the cold, the cracks in both—with the grace they deserved.

The fracture down the lamps center wasn't just failure. It was a reminder.

She let out a slow breath and stepped outside, passing the kids as they tumbled and wrestled on the tundra grass. The sun was just beginning to set, low and stubborn against the horizon. A full month of darkness was coming.

Winter prep had begun.

Tamar joined River near the center of the village where the tribe had gathered around a wide fire pit made from a salvaged shuttle engine. It burned with oil they'd stored from the same shuttle and lit each evening when the wind calmed, making transfer fires easy for the entire community.

She stood beside River, but felt a mile away. He barely even glanced her way. They weren't fighting, not really. But his silence pressed at her, right in the chest.

Why was he doing this? Was she such a failure as an artic woman, he couldn't stand her anymore? Did he wish he was with someone else?

Duncan stood at the front of the fire. Story time.

Tamar's favorite part of the day. A chance to breathe, to listen, to bond with the community. The kids either settled in to listen or darted around behind them, chasing each other in the moonlight.

Families rushed to spread their polar bear pallets, but left the frontmost spot open.

Kallik's spot.

Duncan held out his open hand for River to take it, but he shook his head. Their friends called him out, egging him on. Mostly Big John and Carson.

"Come on," Tamar bumped his shoulder. "It'll at least be cool for the kids."

River sighed and sat. It wasn't *that* big a deal. Their family always sat in the front near Kallik anyway. But Tamar knew—for her husband, it was the gesture. The implication. That he might be stepping into Kallik's place. And that was what made him hesitate.

Tamar glanced back at Takumi and his group. He was staring at River, skewering him with his eyes, but the moment he caught Tamar's gaze, he grinned with his perfect white teeth and waved.

Duncan cleared his throat to begin, and the crowd fell quiet. Bly peeled away from the noisy kids and climbed into her father's lap. River kissed her on the top of her head.

"It was the day—" Duncan spread his hands wide, fire behind him and face alight with drama. "—the First Throne attacked!"

Oh, this was River's favorite.

At first, it had been nearly impossible to get him to come out and sit with the group. He'd complained for weeks. Tamar had to lecture him constantly. "It'll look bad if we're the only family not there."

And he'd always mutter back, "What do I care what people think?"

He hadn't even wanted her to go. He just wanted her in the tent with him.

But slowly, she got him to come. And now? Now he was grinning like a fool, fully into it.

"Jeb loaded the truck with supplies," Duncan said, slipping into his rhythm. "Then his brothers joined him."

"Daddy," Bly whispered. "What's a truck?"

A truck… How would either of them explain that? It had been so long since anyone saw one.

"It's like a giant sled," River murmured to her, "but with wheels. And people didn't have to push it."

"Will you show me one someday?"

"They don't exist anymore, Baby Girl. Let's just listen."

Duncan had clearly remembered new details or maybe just made them up. Every telling changed. Either his memory was improving, or it was his imagination.

Tamar glanced back at Heilo now and then, keeping an eye on him as he roughhoused with the other kids in the back. He'd never cared much for stories.

Jason crouched low and squeezed past a few people to hand River a tusk bone cup. "Try it," he said.

River peered inside, sniffed, and recoiled. "Whoa. I don't think so." He blinked hard, like his eyes burned just smelling it, and handed the cup back.

"Come on… I know what I'm doing."

"No thank you. I'd rather not go blind."

"But you're Pack Leader now. No one will try it unless you do."

"I am not. Go see if Kallik will try it."

"But the cup has your name on it." Jason turned it around, revealing the name *River* etched into the side in childlike scrawl.

River gritted his teeth. “You’re *ruining* the story.”

Jason’s shoulders sagged, and his bottom lip puffed out. It was such a sad sight, tugging at Tamar’s heart. Jason had put a lot of effort into the terrible idea of moonshine.

She bumped River with her shoulder and nodded to Jason, who was already slinking off.

River followed her gaze, and let his head fall back with a groan like the weight of the world was just *too* much. He stood—prompting Duncan to pause mid-story—and stepped up to the fire to whisper in Duncan’s ear.

Duncan raised his eyebrows. River gave a resigned nod.

“Looks like we have an announcement,” Duncan said, grinning. “For tonight only, the role of Pack Leader will be given to Jason.”

River sat back down, smirking.

“Seriously?” Jason blurted, glancing at River, who nodded.

The community burst into cheers, clapping and whistling.

“Way to go, Jason!” Tamar called out with a laugh.

River returned to his seat but shifted over, giving Jason the best spot. Jason lit up like it was the best day of his life. He raised the cup with River’s name high.

“But first—a toast!” he called.

The group fell quiet.

“To River… the best Pack Leader there ever was.”

A wave of laughter rolled through the front half of the camp. Several people raised their fists. “To River!”

But the other half—those sitting near Takumi and Arnaq—remained silent. They watched, firelight flickering across their stony faces.

Jason chuckled and tossed back his concoction.

“I guess I’ve already been forgotten,” a gruff voice called out.

The circle hushed as Kallik stepped into the light, one arm in a sling, the other leaning on Laney for support. River stood, offering his seat and gesturing for others to make room.

Kallik waved him off. "No, no, I'm only teasing."

People scooted and shifted, making space around the front. Kallik settled beside Jason and clapped him on the back.

"So we've got a new hunt leader, huh?" he said with a grin. "River's had enough already?"

Laughter rippled through the circle.

River folded his arms. "How are you feeling?"

"Alive and grateful. Sit." He gestured to the spot next to him, and River obeyed. Tamar slid in next to him, as Bly ran off to join Heilo and the others.

"Let the story continue," Kallik said, raising both hands in mock ceremony.

Duncan made an explosion sound and launched back into the tale, drawing chuckles from the kids and murmured appreciation from the adults. As the background swelled with Duncan's theatrics, Kallik leaned toward River. "I'm thinking of retiring."

River's eyes widened.

Retirement wasn't a bad idea. Elders didn't have to hunt or sew. Their job was to help teach the young and to remember the past.

"If I do, the elders will pick a new Pack Leader," Kallik murmured. "I'm nominating you. But we all know Takumi's going to be a problem."

"I can handle him," River said without hesitation.

"You say that," Kallik replied, "but disharmony in the camp could tear at the structure holding us together. And if that breaks… people *starve*." The last word was gruff and harsh.

River didn't answer. He didn't need to. The fire cracked softly with the background excitement of Duncan's voice.

"The other elders think choosing Takumi will prevent that," Kallik added.

River scoffed. "So he gets his way because he's a giant toddler?"

"That's what I said." Kallik raised his hand with a dry

smile. "Well, not in those words, of course. Still, we are all in agreement. You are going to have to bring him to your side."

"That's not possible."

"Then Takumi *should* be the new hunt leader since you seem unable to inspire confidence in your team."

"What am I supposed to do, beat the snot out of him?"

"Is that the only way you know how to gain cooperation? With violence?"

Tamar couldn't help herself. She snorted.

River narrowed his eyes in her direction—just briefly—to let her know he'd heard.

"You have until winter," Kallik said. He leaned back with a smile. "Now let's sit back and enjoy this wonderful story."

River stared ahead, enthusiasm flickering in Duncan's eyes.

Duncan raised his fist. "Wolverines!"

"Wolverines!" the community shouted back.

Heilo yelped as he rushed past Duncan, clutching something. A dried fish?

A blur snapped through the air. A rope looped around Heilo's waist and yanked him backward chocking another yelp from him. Dirt and dead grass puffed up as he hit the ground laughing.

Big John sauntered over to him, lasso in hand, chuckling. "Little fish thief." He let the rope go slack and held out a hand to receive his prize.

Heilo wriggled free of the rope and raised the fish like a trophy. "Told you I could do it!"

The other kids cheered as he handed the fish back to Big John, then broke into a triumphant dance.

Tamar raised an eyebrow. "Do you always rope children mid-theft?" she called out from her seat.

"Only the fast ones," Big John said, tipping an invisible hat as he wound the rope around his arm.

A smaller boy slung an arm over Heilo's shoulders. "Next

time you got to get *past* the fire pit."

"Easy peasy," Heilo shot back, hand on his hip with a snap of his fingers.

Tamar watched her son run off with the others kids as Duncan got back into his story, then glanced at River with a smile.

"What?" he asked.

"That was a nice thing you did for Jason."

"Nah." He waved a hand. "It was nothing. He has his place here."

She watched Jason passing around the moonshine, sharing and laughing with everyone. "Yes. He does." Then, she rested her head on River's shoulder. "It's nice, isn't it?"

"The story?"

"No. This. Being part of a community. We never had this before. Everyone looks out for each other. No one's left out. No one's unloved. It wasn't like this in the old world."

She paused, squeezing his upper arm. "There's just one word for it."

He hiked his eyebrows at her. "Oh yeah? What's that?"

"Perfection."

He laced his fingers through hers and gave her hand a gentle squeeze. A smile tugging at his mouth.

❄

River stood at the crest of a hill, overlooking the tundra plain in the morning sun. He popped the magazine from his handgun and checked the ammo, as if some might've magically appeared overnight.

Ginger came up behind him, her hair long, light brown hair on top and apple-red ombre at the ends. A heavy supply bag was slung over her shoulder. "Someone call for a blacksmith?"

River moved into her stride with a grin. “I was starting to wonder if you’d ever show.”

“Whatever, Snow Rabbit. You can’t rush greatness.”

River curled his lip. “Don’t tell me that name’s catching on.”

She flashed a devious grin. “You bet your caribou hide it is. Can’t breed like a rabbit without getting called one.”

“Why can’t I have a cool nickname?”

“You prefer Wet Willy? Like Dex?”

River grimaced. “That one stuck too?”

“The worse the nickname, the more likely it is to live forever.”

“Then I better come up with something really awful for you.”

“Not a chance. I’m way too awesome.” She lifted her chin in mock pride.

River glanced at the pack bouncing on her back. “Want me to take that?”

“Don’t you pull that masculinity crap on me.”

“Oh-kay. Should have known,” he said with a laugh. “Tamar missed you last night.”

“Just Tamar?”

He rolled his eyes. “*We* missed you.”

“Noah wanted to turn in early. The hunt wore him out. How are the kids holding up?”

“They’re good.” He slowed, matching her steps. “Still no luck for you two, huh?”

She shook her head, mouth pulling into a frown.

“It’ll happen. You just have to be patient.”

“I’m tired of being told that. You and Tamar didn’t have to wait. Wouldn’t surprise me if she’s expecting again by next season.”

He raised a brow and smirked. “Wouldn’t surprise me either.”

“Yeah—see, that’s disgusting.”

He snickered.

"I never thought I'd be the kind of woman who wants kids so badly," she mumbled.

"This new world's changed us all in ways we didn't expect."

"I used to have machines to fill my time," she said, walking backward. She lifted her hands, as if holding something invisible. "Oh, how I miss the joy of building something with my own hands." She let them fall. "I guess now I just want to build a human. Because that's all I *can* do…You still haven't said anything to Tamar, right?"

"That you want a baby? No. Not like it matters. I don't know why you asked me not to."

"You don't know what it's like," she continued. "When you can't have kids, and your best friend's popping them out left and right. I can't help but be jealous. For our friendship to survive, she has to think I don't *want* them. She can't know I *can't*."

"Maybe it's not Tamar," River said. "Ever think of that?"

"Oh yes, River—the virile stud. Women journey from afar just to beg for his seed." She threw a hand in the air. "Is that what you want to be known for?"

"Who wouldn't?" He grinned.

"This is why half the Pack hates you, you know that, right?"

"Because my masculinity is too much for them?"

"If you think cockiness counts as masculinity. I've known plenty of cocky women."

"Still—the term kind of implies masculism, doesn't it?"

Ginger raised her upper lip. "I guess so. If you're okay being compared to a rooster."

"Are you calling me a chicken?"

"Actually… if I had to pick—I'd call you a hen."

"Oh, I *have* to hear this."

Ginger grinned. "Hear me out. You're rough around the

edges, sure—but you prefer the company of women—to the company of men."

River paused, blinking several times. "You've noticed."

"All your friends are women."

"Kallik?"

"Yes, wise and meek, mild-mannered Kallik fits *right in* with the kindergarten circus that is the hunting team."

"True."

"Which leads to my point. You're going to have to become one of the guys if you're going to manage them."

River rolled his eyes. "But men are idiots."

"Aww, you see?" She patted his shoulder, wiping away an invisible tear. "This is why we're friends."

They both chuckled.

Ginger pulled some dried meat from her pack and handed him a piece. River didn't usually accept food from others, but he knew Ginger was careful with hers, so he took it.

Up ahead, lay the carcass of their old shuttle, long stripped for parts. Its frame sagged, peeled open, a gutted machine half-swallowed by earth and time.

This was a different kind of hunt.

As they wandered through the shuttles graveyard, River scanned every scrape, every warped panel.

"Most of the good metal's already gone," Ginger said, nudging debris with the toe of her caribou kamik.

River lifted a sheet of white plastic shielding, half-burned and warped. *There's got to be more. Just a little more.*

They dug for a while, shifting rubble, flipping charred plates.

"What about this one?" He held up a slender beam.

"Too small. Might be able to make tongs out of it, though. Give me that—Kaya needs one."

He passed it to her and went back to brushing grass around. Ginger tossed heat-scarred shielding off to the side. "Why can't a woman be on the hunting team?"

"I never said one couldn't."

"But there aren't any."

"Do you want to be on it?"

Ginger scoffed. "Getting me to eat fish was enough of a capitulation."

"Hard to be vegan here, huh?"

She gave him a serious look. "So if Bly wanted to be on the hunting team, you'd let her?"

He narrowed his eyes. "*Let* her?"

"You know what I mean."

"I'd be *thrilled* to have her on the team. But chances are, she'll watch her mama sew—and that's what she'll want to do. Nothing wrong with that."

"If I have a boy, I'm getting him into sewing. Like Jason and Oliver."

"Good luck with that." He smirked. "I thought the whole point was that no one gets forced into anything." *Heilo* however, was different. He had to do what kept him safe. But that was a conversation not worth having here.

A sharp glint flashed nearby as he knelt beside a pile of scorched scrap. "I think I found one."

She walked over and kneeled down to inspect it, clearing grass and dirt off. "Yeah. This'll do."

"Need anything to get started?"

"I'm going to need the small jet engine. Do you remember who has it?"

He tilted his head to her. "Who else is the pack rat of the camp?"

"Oliver," they both said in unison.

River rolled his eyes. "I'll get it from him when I get back to the village. Need any more help?"

"I work better alone, but thanks." She stood up, dusting her hands off. "Actually… I think this is enough for two."

River picked it up from the ground and lifted it onto his shoulder. They headed back the way they came. "Then let's make double," he suggested.

"It'll take at least a month. Maybe two."

"So… four hunting trips."

Ginger nodded.

"Tamar will make yours and Noah's meals in the meantime," River added, "so you don't have to."

"This was her idea, right?"

"You think I'd volunteer my wife without asking her first?"

Ginger paused. "I'm surprised she offered. She seems to be having a hard time… You both do."

He didn't respond.

She was pushing and he knew it. Everyone in the community knew things weren't right between them. And normally, he'd talk to Ginger about anything. But not this.

Risking her telling Tamar what he'd overheard her say… He couldn't even *think* about it without his chest tightening. He quickly shut the thought down.

Ginger watched him. "You okay? You got quiet all of a sudden."

Too late.

He scrambled for a change of subject, glancing back at the wreckage. "Looks like the blacksmith's out of a job. You joining the sewers?"

"No way. People'll still need their tools mended."

"Aww. And here I was looking forward to seeing you with a needle in hand."

She frowned.

"You might as well complete the whole package. Homemaker Ginger. I'll even have someone stitch you a pretty frilly apron."

Her shoulders dropped with weariness and exhaustion. "You're a special kind of a-hole, you know that?"

He laughed, slowing his pace with hers. He almost said something cruel—*better than being married to a weakling*—but stopped himself.

That wasn't fair to Noah. He didn't know why it even popped into his head.

"Tell Tamar I said hi," Ginger called after him. "And we'll appreciate the meals."

"Got it. Let me know if I can do more to help."

He handed over the metal. She strapped it to her huge pack, and they parted ways.

River walked backwards a few paces, pointing to his own head. "You know, I've been thinking, the brown hair—it's a good look for you."

She smiled. "Why, River. Are you actually capable of a compliment?"

"Consider it payment for the swords."

She scrunched her face. "I think I'm getting ripped off."

He puffed out his chest, spread his hands wide and mouthed: *Whaat?*

She laughed and shook her head.

He grinned and turned back toward home.

❦❄❦

"You know he's with her right now?" Arnaq said. "They're smiling. And laughing with each other."

"Stop spying on him." Tamar rushed over to pull the canvas flap of their tent away from her, but—too late—she saw it too.

Her stomach dropped.

That smile. She hadn't seen that smile from River in a long time. He hadn't looked at *her* like that in forever.

"And you're okay with this?"

"He said there's nothing going on."

"What else *would* he say? Have you talked to Ginger?"

Tamar shook her head. "She'll just lie too. Won't she?" Tamar loved her friend, but she also knew her temptations.

Other women's husbands were definitely one of them.

"Everyone thinks something's going on between them and you're not doing anything?"

"I'm watching. I'm asking questions. What more can I do?" The pain gnawed at her. Hurtful. Bitter. It scraped her raw inside.

She just wanted it to stop. But what could she do to make it?

Arnaq placed a hand on her shoulder. "Call him out. In the open. Even if it's nothing, the shame will keep them apart. And if it's real, and it gets exposed, he'll be hated. Maybe even banished."

Tamar pictured it. River, knowing what everyone was thinking, attempting to see Ginger in private. And that act being what actually pushed them into each other's arms.

River—banished.

Alone out there… that was death.

"No!" Tamar slapped Arnaq's hand off her shoulder. Arnaq flinched, stepping back.

Tamar buried her face in her hands, trying not to cry. "Please… just leave me alone."

Arnaq didn't reply. Tamar only heard her footsteps as she left.

She sat in the quiet of their home, cradling her qulliq in her hands, running the thumb over its crack.

Duncan's Journal - Week Seven of Midnight Sun

Marital problems happen. Often.
And when they do, there's nowhere to escape your spouse—unless they're on the hunting team. By the time the trip's over, whatever you were fighting about usually doesn't matter anymore.
Distance makes the heart grow fonder…
I wonder if intimate relationships evolved with that tension in mind. Being stuck close to someone with no space—no reprieve—even the strongest couples crack. We're fallible. We're not always kind, or patient, or say the right things.
Expecting anything else is just… unrealistic.
That's probably why my last three marriages failed.
Only being gone for work each day wasn't enough space.
But with Osha, it's different.
I think it's her quiet.
She doesn't talk much. And I don't ask her to.
She doesn't know the deep parts of me.
And I don't know hers.
You'd think that would feel lonely.

But in my other marriages—my wives knew me.

I was definitely still alone.

Every day, we sit and watch the children play.

And aside from the occasional comment—how tall one's gotten, how quickly they've grown—we say nothing at all.

And it's beautiful.

Imagine that.

A partner you can sit beside in perfect peace. No tension. No noise. Just... quiet.

She really is my perfect match.

And she was here, waiting for me all along.

Five

"DON'T," RIVER WARNED.

Tamar swung anyway. He blocked. She fired twice more. Blocked.

She kicked for his hip. But he caught her leg.

Crap.

He attempted to sweep her planted foot, but she saved herself with a hop. He shoved her back using the leg he held, and she lost her balance, hitting the ground.

Every time he got her down in training, it was over. He was too fast.

But not today.

On her side, she went for his knee with a sharp kick. With another assailant, she would have gone straight for the groin. But not on him.

She had other plans for that part of him.

He would have caught her foot again anyway.

He blocked her kick with his shin and then he was on her. Straddling her. He caught her wrists and pinned them above her head, pressing them into the tundra.

He stared down at her with those piercing blue eyes.

Tamar's breath caught.

It was the position. The control. The heat of him. The strength she hadn't felt in too long. He held her there easily, heavy breaths slipping past his parted lips.

And for a split second, something shifted in his expression. Like he felt it too. Like they might just close the distance and forget everything.

But he leaned back. Space returned between them.

That hurt more than the fall.

She had missed this. Missed his hands on her. Missed the way he used to lean in and soften instead of pulling away.

Now there was no softness. Only restraint.

She forced her breathing steady, refusing to let him see how much she still wanted him.

"How are you going to get me off of you?" he huffed.

Who says I want to? The words hovered on the edge of her tongue.

But the risk of him pulling back, of shutting that door on her, wasn't something she could bare.

She tried to spin her wrists to release his grip, but couldn't. He was way too strong, and growing stronger with each hunt.

"Get me off of you," he growled.

"I can't!" she wailed.

"Yes, you can. Come on, Tamar."

His weight pressed down on her. Solid. Unyielding...

Distractingly solid. With very unfair arm muscles that—

STOP.

Focus.

It had to be the head. *Oh.* She hated to do this to him.

Using her forehead, she popped him in the nose. He reared back with a cry. She brought her thumb joints in and flung her hands to her sides, releasing his grip.

She had to be fast. She had to be quick.

With her elbows at her sides, she grabbed his forearm, placed all five fingers over his wrist and pushed up with her hips, using the ground as leverage.

It felt like the right move. In more ways than one—thrusting into him like that.

Thoughts…on the training, she screamed at herself.

He was forced to roll over her and now she was on top. With two fingers, she jabbed toward the spot below his Adam's apple, right above the "V" on his collarbone.

He slapped her hand away and lunged forward with his hand on her shoulders to throw her. Instinctively, she drove her elbow into the side of his head, right in his temple.

He yelped—more grunt than cry—and dropped back.

"Are you okay?" She clapped a hand over her mouth.

He clutched his head where she'd hit him. "Don't. Stop."

She nodded and drove her fist into his gut. The breath burst out of him in a sharp bark. His body tightened beneath her, abdominal muscles locking as he tried to absorb the blow.

Before he could recover, she shifted her weight forward, planted a hand on his chest, and rolled off to his side. She came up low into a crouch, pivoting as he twisted to face her.

She attempted to strike at his ribs as he turned. River sucked in a breath through his teeth, then popped his legs under him and sprang upright in one fluid motion, avoiding her leg.

She rose with him, settling into a firm defensive stance.

They faced each other. Locked. Still. A standoff.

He never made the first move. Ever.

He'd stand there all day if he had to, unmoving, unreadable. His opponent was always the one to break. Which at that moment—was her.

Holding their stances, they stared at each other. There was a reason he did. He'd never told her, but after years of lessons from him, she'd finally figured it out.

To attack meant leaving yourself open.

She preferred to be on offensive. It meant control, dictating tempo and setting the overall mood of the fight.

But a first strike divided focus. You lost attention to defense. You gave yourself away.

You telegraphed your moves.

That was why she couldn't beat him. Because River never

attacked first. He waited. Let you open up, then struck at the fault line.

That was the point where she would have to strike, to get him where he thought she was open. To feign it. That meant seeing his moves—three moves in advance.

It was a chess game. Fighting was simply a chess game. That's all it was. A chess game with their bodies.

He sighed, sunlight glinting off his dark hair, tied back from his face. "We going to stand here all day?"

She feigned like she was going to kick, which unfortunately wasted a bit of energy. He low-blocked with his forearm like expected and kicked, no doubt noticing the opening she left for him.

Quickly—she slid between his legs, grabbing the grounded foot as she glided across the loose dirt. And since his other leg was up for a kick, he fell forward with a thud.

She crawled over his back and did a pretend knife stab right where his heart would be. "You're dead," she whispered right in his ear.

A grin swept over his face as he got up and dusted the dirt off his arms. "Took you long enough."

"I could never see if before." She held her hands out in disbelief. "I thought fighting was all about being stronger or faster, mindless rage taking over. But it's not at all."

"Nope."

"Why didn't you just tell me?"

"And rob you of this moment? It's not the same as seeing it for yourself."

It was as if her eyes had been opened. It was all about balance. Balancing the offensive with the defensive.

Which was true in everything in life, relationships, communication, work and play, *everything.*

Harmony, that was what it was.

And he just taught her that, without saying a word.

He sat there, watching her. Something in his eyes shifted,

too quiet, too guarded.

She felt the pull in her chest.

For a heartbeat, she thought he might reach for her. Pull her in. Let the lesson end differently.

But he didn't.

The harmony between them was missing.

He hunched over, resting with his hands on his knees. "You beat me because you've learned to predict my moves over the years. It won't be the same with an unknown opponent, so don't get cocky. Don't underestimate. Always stay vigilant and watch what their movements tell you."

She nodded, watching the camp from afar. The men were collecting, waiting for him. "I hate when you leave..."

It slipped out. Too tender for the moment.

But this was the first hunt without Kallik. With River solely in charge.

He rose, brushing the grass off his hide pants, gaze fixed on the horizon like he hadn't heard her at all. Combing his fingers through his hair, grabbing the hairs that had come loose, he retied it back in a nob. "We need to talk about Heilo's arrangement."

Not that again. She crossed her arms and leaned away from him.

"Marriage is not a choice out here, it is a necessity," he pressed as he stepped closer to her.

"Are you going to control everything about his life? It seems like the kind of thing that should be his choice."

"The world has changed. The old world is dead. Those kinds of luxuries no longer exist. And pretending they do, won't make it so."

She squeezed her eyes shut. This was their son's life they were playing with, his future. And now it felt like a decision on a ledger. "It's not like love matches are unheard of."

"True. But all the kids his age are arranged, except him and Harkin's daughter. Harkin and Kaya are waiting on us and the community is expecting us to do it."

"But what if he doesn't like her?"

"He'll adapt. And honestly—it's more likely she won't like *him.*"

"Not like Heilo? Never."

River scoffed. "Didn't think you'd be one of *those* mothers."

"What is that supposed to mean?"

"You don't think anyone is good enough for your *baby boy.*"

"Well… they aren't." Tamar tilted her head away.

River narrowed his eyes. "You're going to need to get over that. Do you want him to be alone?"

She knew he was right. And if they asked Heilo right now, he'd probably agree without hesitation. But he was just a boy. What if he resented the decision later? She didn't want to hold that kind of power over his future. If they got it wrong, the guilt would eat her alive. "It's just—why do we have to talk about this right now? He's still a boy."

"He won't stay one."

"He's got plenty of time."

River shook his head. "And what if Emma's baby is a boy? Harkin and Kaya might pair Tulah with him instead, out of frustration with how long we're taking, and Heilo ends up with no one. Is that what you want?"

"And what if the baby's a girl?" she countered. "Heilo would have more choices."

River's jaw clenched. "Is that a risk you're willing to take?"

"Everything's a risk," Tamar said. "We live with risk every day. Every time you leave, something could happen to us and you wouldn't know until you got back."

He crossed his arms and squared his shoulders. "You would think that you wouldn't leave the camp without me then."

Oh gosh. Not this.

Nice segue. He'd probably been waiting all morning for that opening.

She didn't respond, just walked forwad, hoping he'd let it die.

He didn't.

"You've got nothing to say to that?"

"I didn't think your statement solicited a response."

She was nearly back to the village. River caught up, grabbing both her arms and forcing her to face him. "Do *not* leave the camp again without me."

She pulled herself free. "I think I proved today that I can take care of myself."

"And what did I say about getting cocky?" His voice rose. "That's *exactly* how it happens. You start believing you're invincible—and then *bam*." He smacked his fist into his palm. "You're dead."

She shook her head. "I never said I was invincible."

He rubbed his temple with one hand, exasperated. "Don't leave the camp without me," he hissed, slicing the air with his other hand for emphasis. He jogged ahead to grab his pack he had left before training, and joining the other hunters waiting near the village edge before she could reply.

Tamar let out a long breath as she watched him leave. She hated arguing before a hunt. But sometimes, it just… couldn't be helped.

❄

"Carson and Kodik, tie the ropes," River said, stabbing his spear into the snow. The team was far from home and at a higher elevation.

"Fine," Kodik grumbled, yanking the rope from Takumi. "But Carson's knots come undone if you so much as look at them wrong."

"That's 'cause your face is so ugly it scares them," Carson shot back.

"Knock it off," River said in a whisper shout. "You *idiots* are being too loud."

Big John crouched by the kill, studying it. "This bull's massive."

"Pretty sure we're close to wolf territory," Dex murmured to Takumi, who nodded.

Takumi unrolled the drag canvas, already stiff with dried blood. "This thing's about had it." He held it up. Torn, tattered, thin enough to see through.

"We've got a backup, right?" Big John asked.

"Yeah, but two trips with one canvas? That's a lot of wasted skin."

River shook his head. "That's not sustainable."

Kodik stood, finishing the knots. "We could go back to using the travois."

"Aww, I *hate* the travois," Carson whined.

"Shut up, Carson," Takumi growled, glaring him down.

Big John chuckled. "You're not getting a four-hundred-pound bull on a travois."

Takumi crossed his arms. "We wouldn't have this problem if we had dogs."

Kodik rolled his eyes. "Not this again." He stepped closer, gesturing wildly. "We don't have dogs. Get over it."

"We looking at what…" Big John rubbed his chin. "Two-hundred and forty pounds of boneless meat?"

Dex spat on the ground. "Give or take."

"Gut on-site?" Kodik suggested.

"You're going to gut near wolf territory?" Takumi shook his head. "That's risky."

"So is dragging a bull this big back home," Big John said as he crossed his arms.

Takumi bit his lip and scanned the horizon. "This warm summer's pushing the big ones higher. We ain't gonna starve this winter."

The conversation fell, and River waited. He studied Takumi, who was still chewing his bottom lip.

Fine. He'd try it Kallik's way.

"What do you think we should do?" he asked him.

Takumi's eyes narrowed. A slow, obnoxious smirk curled his mouth. "Can't make the decision yourself, huh?"

River grinned back, with a short exhale "What idiot wouldn't ask the wolf expert his advice near wolf territory?"

Takumi's shoulders lifted. "Maybe the wolf expert should just take over this whole operation—since you're clearly unqualified."

The entire pack went quiet. Watching them. Tension snapped through the air, pulled tight like a gut string about to break in all their faces.

Of course, the giant toddler was going to make this hard. "Big John." River didn't break eye contact with Takumi. "How long to build a travois?"

"Just need the poles. Give me ten minutes."

The tree line was in sight. River stepped in close to Takumi, chest out, eyes narrowing. "Go with Big John and get it built. Think you can handle that?"

Takumi grinned wide—too wide—and scanned River before walking off without a word.

"Dex, Upa, Zack, and Nukilik, stand guard," River said while pointing a spear at each of them. The men took off, spreading out in a five-star perimeter.

"Oh no. No no," Carson whined.

"Yep. Carson, Kodik and Noah, get to gutting."

Not two seconds later, Nukilik shouts. "Bear!"

River took off running toward him, then skidded to a stop as the rest of the pack followed.

"That's—not a polar bear," Kodik said, voice thin.

From behind a rocky hill, the creature emerged, about ten yards out. It was the size of a bear.

White fur rippled over thick muscle, and a rough mane circled its head. But its face was flat. No snout. Just bared, serrated teeth under two dark, soulless eyes. Its front paws curled under, knuckle-walking with weight and power. Its back hunched like a white gorilla.

"Kill it," River growled, harsh but calm. Arrows flew.

The creature turned and bolted, an arrow buried deep in its back. River chased it until it reached the water's edge, where it dove and disappeared.

The rest of the hunters caught up, breathless, shaking their heads in disbelief.

"What was that?" Kodik huffed.

"Some type of mutation?" Noah offered. "I've never seen anything like it before."

Carson clapped his hands and pointed at Kodik. "I know! It was a Yeti."

Kodik shook his head. "There's no such thing as Yetis."

Carson threw his hands out, eyes wide. "Of course, there is! How else do you explain that thing?"

"Ever heard of a Yeti crawling on its front paws like a sloth?" Kodik shot back.

"Maybe it's a *deformed* Yeti," Carson said, grinning. "Like your sister."

Kodik smacked him across the back of the head.

"It wasn't a yeti," River whispered. He crouched near the water, still watching where it had vanished, not ready to turn his back to it.

An unspoken sentiment moved across the team and everyone was quiet.

River's jaw tightened. It wasn't a yeti…

Duncan's Journal - Days of Lingering Light

I try not to think about the Avalon Project.
But I do.
There are too many questions—ones no one will ever answer.
It's maddening.

If I had one wish, it wouldn't be for peace, or longevity, or even love.
It would be to know what happened there.
What really happened.

Sometimes I wonder if Earth has a failsafe—
a self-correcting mechanism that activates when we get too close to breaking free.
Maybe every time we reach for the stars, the planet shifts beneath us.
Continents move. Systems collapse. Memory fails.

I call it the World Changing Theory.
We rise.
We fall.
We don't leave.
We reset.
Again and again.

Maybe the Avalon Project wasn't a breakthrough.
Maybe it was a warning.

Six

ARNAQ SLUNG AN arm around Tamar's shoulders. "Oh, my sweet, gullible friend—give *him* the silent treatment back."

The other sewers nodded in agreement, even Jason and Oliver, while the last warm glow of evening clung to the horizon.

"Why bother if he's not even trying?" said Ana, with her middle-aged brow arched in judgment.

Tamar chewed on her bottom lip. "I don't know. I just thought… maybe being cold wouldn't help anything."

Arnaq leaned away from her, arms crossed, hip cocked. "And being nice is?"

"No."

"You've tried talking to him, right? He shuts down?" She lifted both palms up.

Tamar didn't answer. Just stared at the pants she'd nearly finished stitching—River's pants—with their uneven stitches.

Did he still belong to her? Did he still have romantic feelings for her? Lately, it hadn't felt like it. And Arnaq's reasoning… made too much sense.

Maybe it was time he got a taste of his own medicine.

"What choice has he left you?" Arnaq asked. The rest of the circle murmured their agreement.

Several small black dots emerged on the horizon, just beyond where the sewers worked in the amber glow of the

setting sun. River must have pushed the team hard, determined not to camp overnight. Kallik would have stopped.

As the figures drew closer, Tamar made out the Pack hauling a loaded travois, with two smaller caribou slung across Takumi and Kodik's shoulders. A successful hunt.

They had maybe an hour and a half before the daylight gave out. Dividing the haul would have to be quick. Tamar's heart sank as the frustration she'd shoved aside for the past two weeks clawed its way back up.

Her husband was home.

Fine. If distance was what he wanted, she could give that too.

The hunters dragged the kills into the circle and dropped to their knees as the singing began. River took off his gloves and sat on them, settling into his routine.

But Tamar didn't sit across from him.

Not this time.

She stood for a moment, watching the sun cast red and gold across his face. Then she gave him one glance—tired and done.

And walked away.

Past the bull. Toward Arnaq and Takumi.

Takumi looked up with a grin. "Joining the A team?"

She let out a soft laugh. "I'm anything but the A team." Then she knelt beside them, pulled her knife, and got to work.

River didn't move. Didn't blink. Didn't seem to even breathe.

Takumi, of course, noticed. He carved a raw strip of caribou, lifted it with two fingers, and ate it slow. Never breaking eye contact with River. It was a tradition that always turned her husband's stomach.

But this time, Tamar didn't care. She even smirked at Takumi for it, just a flick of amusement. He lit up like he'd been handed a gift, chewing slow, eyes gleaming with something halfway between triumph and trouble.

"Dude, I hate it when you do that," Carson called across the kill. "How does that not make you sick?"

"Muscle is sterile, you slush-brained moose tick," Takumi shot back. "As if half of you didn't eat rare steaks before the Disaster. No different."

River said nothing. His jaw locked tight.

Once the work was done, the community dispersed, each family hauling meat and furs back to their shelters.

The kids trailed Tamar as she carried the furs, River following behind with the meat. He carried it behind the canvas door, setting it down with a heavy thud. His jaw flexed.

"What do you think it says when my own wife chooses to sit with *him* instead of me?" He didn't say his name directly, as if doing so was some kind of sacrilege.

His voice cracked at the edge, but his glare stayed cold. "Do you even realize what you've done?"

"I wasn't sitting *with* him—I was sitting with *my friend*."

"I don't want him near my family." He pointed at her, finger still streaked with blood. "Not the kids. Not you."

"Well that's going to be a little difficult since he's—*in our community!*" the last part she shouted. She didn't care that the whole camp heard, let them.

"He's the closest thing I have to an enemy, and you're over there *laughing* with him like he's some friend of yours."

"He's married to one of my closest friends, *that's* all. And you'd probably have no problem getting along with him if you'd just learn to stop scowling at people every time they breathed."

River's hand sliced the air. "You have no idea what you're talking about."

"You can believe that if it helps you sleep, but I'm not going to start treating people like garbage just to coddle your insecurities."

"If I'm insecure—" he snapped, "—it's because of *you*."

He kicked her pile of furs over.

She paused, fingers pressed to her temple, and let out a breath through her nose. The kids shouldn't be seeing this. "Of course. All your faults, all your rage, always someone else's doing. But here's the thing, River—your choices? *Still yours.*"

Little Bly raised her arms to ask to be held but tripped on the hardened ground. Her knees scraped raw. She let out a wail, clutching her leg.

"Shh—Bly." Heilo whispered with an eyeroll. "Don't cry. Not now."

"She got hurt, Heilo." Tamar said, voice clipped. "That's allowed."

River stared while Tamar pulled an old fur scrap from her pocket, dabbed Bly's knee, her own heart scraped raw.

They were too young for this—parenthood, marriage, fights that stacked like kindling. Resentment building with no clue how to burn it off without burning down the whole house.

Bly shouldn't have to hear it. Neither should Heilo.

"She's always getting hurt," Heilo muttered, folding his arms. "She's always crying. *Typical* girl."

River grabbed the front of his son's parka with a blood-slicked hand, rage flashing in his eyes. "Don't you talk about your sister like that. Do you understand me?"

Heilo's lips pressed into a hard line. He nodded—stiff, silent—until River let him go.

"Why don't you go play with the others," Tamar said, feeling an urgency to get him away from River as soon as possible.

Heilo turned and left without a word. Tamar scooped up Bly, furs still tucked under one arm, and carried her to her cot.

"Who's he been playing with?" he snapped. "Where would he even pick that up?"

"Maybe from his own father." Tamar laid Bly on the bed, unrolling a worn hide to wrap the scrape. He can't keep blaming other people for his short comings.

River's eyes darkened. "Excuse me?"

It's not the right time for this, but Tamar didn't listen to herself. She was past caring. "I seem to remember a certain boyfriend of mine saying things like that all the time."

"I would never say that."

"Well..." Tamar tilted her head, mouth tugging sideways. "Actually, you did."

"I did not."

She tapped a finger to her cheek, mock thoughtful. "What was it you said? Something about how real men don't need a good cry after?"

"I never said anything like that." He watched her, his eyes firm and contemplating. His voice dropped, rough. "So that's what you really think of me?" He glanced away with a bitter laugh. "It all makes sense now."

She said nothing. The conversation wasn't worth the blood pressure.

He stepped close, low and biting. "It's *him,* isn't it? He's getting into your head."

"Oh right..." She nodded. "Because I'm just some dumb woman who can't make her own decisions? Like I said—*you* are the kind of man who says that. Who thinks that."

She lifted Bly onto her hip and turned toward the door. The tension in the room was too thick, her daughter didn't need to be around it. She had a toddler in one arm and a crumbling husband across the room. No one taught her how to do this part.

River watched her, his teeth grit and eyes furious. "That's *it.*" He flung his hands up. "You never listen. I'm done. I'm not doing this anymore."

"Done how?" Tamar looked back, chin tilted down. "Now you're just being dramatic." She pulled open the canvas door and walked out. Only to stop short.

Heilo stood at the door, wide-eyed and silent. The light from their lamps inside outlining the heartbreak raw in his face. . She reached for his hand and tugged him along.

“Mama…” Heilo’s voice was small. “What did Daddy mean by *done*?”

She knelt beside him and held his arm. “Sweetheart, Daddy shouldn’t have said that. It’s nothing, alright? It will be forgotten about tomorrow. Try not to worry.” Her voice stayed soft, even as her gut twisted.

She spotted Laney and Kallik watching from a distance, their faces unreadable. Great. Another scene.

Tamar rose, keeping Heilo close, and made it for Ginger’s. Anything to get out of the open. Anything to keep this from spiraling more than it already had.

“Are you going to live with Takumi now?” Heilo’s voice wavered. “The other kids said… he’s going to be my new dad.”

The words hit Tamar like ice cracking beneath her feet—sudden, sharp, and full of dread for whatever came next. How could Heilo even *think* such a thing?

“Heilo. Enou—”

Her throat closed. She froze.

Takumi sat in the shadows, pipe in hand, moonlight catching the edge of his cheekbone. He’d heard. Of course he had. Tamar’s face flushed hot.

Had he been listening to their argument the whole time? He stood and sauntered toward them. “Hey, Tamar.”

She inhaled sharply, nodded once, and clutched Heilo’s hand tighter, pulse skittering.

He crouched to Heilo’s level, voice warm. “Hey, little man.”

Heilo didn’t answer.

“It’s been a while since we caught lemmings on the rocks,” Takumi said gently, ruffling his hair. “We should do that again sometime.”

He straightened, pipe at his lips, and met her eyes, longer than he needed to. “What were you two talking about just now?”

“Nothing,” she grit her teeth at him—too fast, too sharp.

She pulled Heilo past him before he could press. Somehow, some way, River always got his way. And it was infuriating.

River sat on the edge of his bed, fists clenched until his knuckles throbbed. Anger twisted in his gut, brittle and ready to snap.

He could hear Takumi's voice outside with hers. Did she run–*to him?*

Didn't she realize how this looked? How it felt?

After she'd sat beside him?

Maybe he shouldn't have said those things. But what was he supposed to do now? Chase after her, beg her forgiveness? That would only make him look weak.

He was losing her a little more each day. It had been his plan, the best way to protect them both, but he hadn't expected it to hurt this much. He'd thought he could handle it.

He'd been wrong.

Takumi envied him because of Tamar. That—he had suspected for years. And up until recently, it never mattered.

But the more she was around him, the more uncompliant Takumi became.

She was making it worse. All he was asking for was a little solidarity. A little help. And that was too much for her to give?

He grabbed a large metal pot and headed to the lagoon for water. He was filthy and still needed to clean up.

Outside, Noah was there watching Heilo play with the other kids, as he slugged and tackled the other boys and two tough younger girls.

Heilo spotted his father and punched Logan, Dex's kid, really hard, like he was showing off then ran up to him. The other boy gave chase but stopped when he saw River.

The front of his son's parka was bloodied from when he'd grabbed him earlier. He shouldn't have grabbed him like that. Heilo was all covered in mud now anyway—but still. That shouldn't have happened. He'll have to clean him up later.

Heilo seemed uncertain, as he watched his father. Probably because of what he said. "It's okay, Heilo. Go on and play." Heilo nodded and ran back off to play with the others.

River returned with the water and set it near the fire to warm. Noah stepped beside him, both of them watching the kids play as the heat rose behind them.

"Tamar's at my house," Noah said.

River blinked, the words throwing off his expectation. He leaned back against the wide aluminum ring, heat licking his spine. Maybe Ginger could talk some sense into her. "Right. I figured."

"The women wanted to talk, so Tamar asked me to take Heilo out."

"Thanks." A long pause followed. River cleaned his teeth with his tongue, watching the shadows from the fire.

Noah leaned toward him. "Good to be home, huh?" His tone had that old familiar snark.

River snorted, shaking his head. "Should've stayed in the wilderness."

"Ain't that the truth."

The night was cooling fast, cutting deeper with every breath. Above them, the sky cracked open in a storm of green fire, aurora borealis flickering like it mattered. Useless beauty for a world that only seemed to tighten around him.

Shouts from the boys stole their attention, as Heilo knocked back an entire dog pile.

"I've got to hand it to you," Noah said, with a snicker. "That's some boy you've got."

River smirked. "In that case, I guess I'll keep him." He did an inner eyeroll to himself. Such a cliched line, but he didn't know what else to say.

A mudball smacked him in the face. Charlie—the youngest of Zack's crew—froze, eyes wide with horror. The other kids stopped what they were doing and stared.

"You hit my dad!" Heilo screeched before slamming into him. The other boys join in too, kicking and screaming.

"Whoa, hey!" River shouted, brushing the mud off his face. "It's okay."

The boys stopped and Heilo shouted, "Now apologize!"

Charlie crept forward, lower lip trembling.

River kneeled down to his level. "Hey, no biggie. It was an accident, right? Why don't you run home and get cleaned up."

The boy nodded and took off. River pointed to Heilo, "You hear that? All is forgiven, now let it go." The small pack scattered back into chaos.

River stood back up into his spot. Noah gave a quick wave with two fingers. "You know, that whole thing that happened with Takumi, whatever that was—I just want you to know… I've got your back."

River's mouth moved to the side, with a humoring smirk and nod, "Thanks Noah. Means a lot."

"It's nothing, I know you'd do anything for me too."

There was an awkward pause, as Noah seemed to be waiting for an affirmation to the comment. But it wasn't true. River wouldn't do *anything* for him.

There were actually very few things he'd do. The only reason both men even seemed to have a connection was because their wives were friends.

"*Don't be unkind unless you have to be*," Tamar's voice echoed. He didn't have to be. So, he said nothing. Just gave a nod that wasn't quite agreement, walking off with his water and headed back to his home.

❄

"I've never seen anything like it," River said, sitting alone with Duncan beneath the clear, crisp stars. The kids had long since fallen asleep.

Its limbs were too long. Its face too flat.

Wrong. That's what it was.

Just like you?

The thought clawed in, uninvited. He shoved it down. They were talking about that—thing.

"There was something about the way it moved, like it didn't belong anywhere. Not even in its own skin."

"Well…" Duncan exhaled slowly, smoke drifting from his pipe. "The planet changed. Stands to reason the wildlife would, too. Ninety-six percent of all species that ever lived have gone extinct. Chances are, this one will follow soon enough."

River shook his head. "Not before I kill it."

"It's an unusual species," Duncan said gently. "Let nature sort it out. At least give the creature a chance."

"So our territory can be overrun by them?" River countered. "We have enough trouble with polar bears."

Duncan rubbed his forehead, frustrated. "It's probably just a mutated bear, and it's likely already suffering."

"Then I'm doing it a favor by ending its misery."

"River—" Duncan's voice tightened, exasperation clear. "Why chase trouble? Do you really need to prove yourself this badly?"

"I don't have anything to prove," River said through clenched teeth. "You didn't see it. You have no idea how dangerous it was."

Duncan sighed heavily. "And if it kills you instead? What happens to Tamar and your kids then?"

Silence stretched between them. River gazed up at the distant, uncaring stars. Usually Duncan made sense, could even talk him down from his worst impulses, but not this time.

River rose sharply, jaw tight, decision made. "It's an abomination. I'm going to hunt it down and kill it."

As he turned away, Duncan murmured just loud enough to be heard, "The line between bravery and stupidity is thin, River."

River kept walking with no doubts.

It had to die.

It was either it, or them.

Duncan's Journal - Days of Lingering Light

River's an idiot.

Seven

FOOTSTEPS CRUNCHED CLOSER as Ginger gave the swords a final polish. She didn't bother looking up—only one person had that gait stride and walked like they owned the planet.

River stood there with that maddening grin of his. The one that said he'd not only caught the fish but convinced it to thank him afterward. "Those mine?"

She tilted her head, giving him a sharp smirk back. "Depends. Planning to use them or just pose shirtless with them?"

"No promises." He placed his hands on his hips, clearly presenting disappointment. "I was hoping they'd be ready."

"They *are*. Barely. I was trying to finish before the ego storm hit."

"It's fine. I'll help." He grabbed a cloth and started polishing.

Ginger blinked. No insult? No clever jab? Does River have an evil twin? Or more like *non-evil* twin?

They finished in a few quiet minutes. She handed it to him and he lifted both blades crossed over each other with theatrical reverence, inspecting them.

So dramatic. After an eye roll, Ginger nibbled her bottom lip. "Noah told me you plan to take them out for the first time on a voluntary hunt to kill that creature."

River scrunched his nose up. "I was really happy to hear he intends to join me."

"Did he tell you how I asked him not to."

"He did."

Ginger exhaled through her nose. "Do you *have* to kill it?"

River didn't flinch. "Not up for debate."

That was fine. She'd already heard both sides: one half of the camp wanted it dead, the other wanted it medium-rare. And River, Mr. Safety Scissors, was firmly in Team: *Do Not Eat the Nightmare Beast*.

The Elders were already making up stories, telling the children it was an *idukupa.* Ready to grab them in their sleep if they didn't behave and keep quiet. Funny how quickly the kids all hopped into bed once nightfall came.

He brought the swords down after one final inspection. "You're good at this."

"I'd hope so. The community always needs tools. Never made a sword before though—kind of winged it."

He did a few showy twirls with both blades, like some kind of tundra action hero.

"All right, Sir Lancelot, we get it," Ginger said. "Still not sure how you plan to *hunt* with one."

River snorted. "It's mostly for when a polar bear gets ambitious and thinks I'm lunch."

Hide straps are pulled out of his belt. He put them around his shoulders, carefully sliding the swords into a X on his back.

Ginger folded her arms. "Y'know, that was the last of the metal. Someone else might've needed a sword also. Do you really need two?"

"One's for Heilo. When he's older." He winked at her with a click of his tongue. "Besides, not like you'd use it. Word is, someone's joining the sewers when not repairing tools. So should I get you that frilly apron or assume you'll stitch it yourself?"

She shrugged. "I'll just use it to strangle you in your sleep."

"Little Miss Mechanic with a needle and thread," River said with a rhythm and a snicker.

"Ha. Ha. Laugh it up, furball."

One side of his face scrunched. "Furball?"

She waved it off. "Movie line."

"I know that one—What was it from?"

She got quiet and watched sadly into the distance. "I don't remember."

River pursed his lips with a nod. "I'll bring over an entire season of hides tomorrow."

Ginger jumped up. "Woo, I think I'm rich!"

"Look around you," he walked off with his hands up, displaying the camp with his hand. "You already were."

❄

"Are you sure these are its tracks?" River asked Big John.

Big John crouched beside the prints, two deep, curved slashes in front, broad polar bear paws in back. "Never seen anything like 'em. What else could it be?"

They'd been tracking it for three days now. The party was small, just those willing. After Duncan's speech, River hadn't wanted to issue an order. This wasn't for food. Plenty of men had stayed home with their families, unwilling to kill a creature that hadn't attacked.

A low snarl stopped them cold.

They crept up over a snowdrift.

The beast was massive, its chest soaked red, muzzle buried in the body of a fallen caribou. It didn't look up. Didn't sense them downwind. An old wound festered on its back where Big John's arrow had hit a week before.

He raised a fist.

The men halted.

He signaled with one hand—up, then forward.

Arrows flew.

One struck its side. The others thudded harmlessly into snow. The beast lifted its bloodied head, bellowed, and bolted downhill toward the water.

"Spears!" River demanded. "Don't let it reach the water!"

They missed. River cursed under his breath. If it made it to the lagoon, it was gone. No one could follow it in, and live.

"Big John, lasso," River shouted, already running.

"From here?" Big John panted, keeping stride.

"I've seen you do twice that!"

Big John skidded to a stop and flung the rope. It hit the ground uselessly.

"Again."

He reeled the rope in, fingers flying. The beast was yards from the shoreline now.

"One more shot," River called.

Big John swung the lasso wide and let it fly.

It caught.

The rope snapped tight around the creature's neck, yanking it down hard. Snow burst skyward as it fell. The beast thrashed and scrambled back up, but Big John dug in, heels anchored.

Two more hunters rushed in with ropes, forming a tight triangle. The creature's panic was unmistakable, breath ragged, eyes wild. It clawed at the air, straining toward the water. So close.

River stepped forward and unsheathed his sword. The creature stilled, eyes locking onto his. No rage. Just fear.

Its chest heaved. One eye half-shut, mouth twitching. River raised the blade, but something in him stalled.

Not out of mercy. Out of recognition.

Get it over with. End it before you see.

A hoarse gasp wheezed from its throat. His own reflection shimmered in its pupils, warped, monstrous.

Was this wrong?

They'd caught it. It wasn't attacking. It was just trying to live. But what if next time, someone didn't make it home? What if it changed?

No one else would've hesitated.

It was those eyes.

Not human. Not animal.

Not right. *Just like him.*

He shook his head in a sharp, violent rhythm. *Not like him.*

Maybe he should just let it go. But if he did and someone died later... that would be on him.

"Better safe than sorry," he murmured.

"What?" another hunter asked.

River didn't answer. Just raised the blade.

At least he could make it quick.

The sword sliced clean across the throat. The creature collapsed, blood steaming on the snow. Its eyes rolled back.

"Die and be in peace," River said, and whipped the blade clean with one hard fling.

Eight

TAMAR SAT SEWING in the sun beside Ginger while Osha and her daughter, Sura, hovered nearby, demonstrating stitches. Ginger, of course, picked it up with obnoxious ease. Tamar had already learned not to compliment her. Ginger hated that.

She shot her a look, smirking at Tamar's uneven threading. "Can you believe this? Us. Married. Sewing. Like a couple of grandmas."

The air cracked. A low boom rolled through the hills, followed by a sharp sonic blast that made every eye turn skyward. A streak of fire tore across the blue, burning white-hot as it split the atmosphere.

Tamar and Ginger jumped to their feet, shielding their eyes as the trail arced toward the horizon. A long, molten scar stretching north.

Another satellite. Which meant—metal.

"Should we go after it?" Osha called, shading her brow from the sun. "We could send the men."

Ginger squinted, tracking the smoke until it vanished into a thin haze above the sea. "No point," she said. "It's heading for the ocean."

Disappointment settled over them. Four or five fell each year, but most hit water or burned away before touching land. The few that didn't, left little more than slag, wire, melted panels, blackened copper, a glint of gold if fortune smiled. Once, they'd found a curved shard of mirror glass big enough to catch the sun. It hung in the Elders meeting tent now, the closest thing they had to proof that the old world had ever existed.

Emma waddled past, belly round and gleaming with sweat, and the conversation died. Both women watched her walk by.

There were so many of them now, young and swelling with new life. It still felt surreal, like they were children playing at adulthood, sewing sunlight into the hems of a world that was still learning how to begin again.

Tamar swallowed, eyes lingering on Emma's back, knowing what was coming for her. It was terrifying being one of the first to go through labor from the Moon Crew.

No hospital. No medicine.

A legacy of woman had already paved the way for safer childbirth, they shouldn't have to regress backward. "This is not how I pictured life after high school," she murmured.

"Raging hormones and zero birth control," Ginger said, stitching clean and fast. "Dream big." She knotted a thread using her teeth. "You gotta wonder…are we heading back to twelve-year-olds having babies?

Tamar shivered. "Hope not."

Ginger went quiet for a moment, then added, "You know, in the old world, you'd have been treated like a cautionary tale for having a kid this young."

Tamar didn't argue. "Yeah. I know." She used to think the same way. Irresponsible. Unfit. A life already halfway over.

"People would've said you ruined your future," Ginger went on. "That your kid deserved better. That you'd probably end up doing it alone."

Tamar shook her head, thinking of Kaya. "It's the same now. Just—your man might die on a hunt."

"I think that's less painful than him leaving."

Tamar let out a soft, disbelieving laugh. "Him dying?"

Ginger didn't flinch. "Yeah. One is grief. The other's rejection."

"I think a lot of widows would disagree with you."

"Maybe. But to have him alive and not want you?" Ginger glanced up. "That cuts deeper."

Tamar nodded slowly. "Yeah… I guess so."

She didn't look at Ginger. Didn't want to. Was that a general truth—or something she knew? Something River told her? Something she was warning Tamar about?

"It's not safe for a woman without community," Tamar said. "I'd never do it alone."

"Why's that?" Ginger asked. "What makes community so special?"

"It keeps people in check. Forces a kind of moral code," Tamar said. "Sounds restrictive, but most people need boundaries. That's all religion is, really."

"Okay, but can't you just set your own?"

"You can. But if you're building something with someone—raising kids, surviving together—you need shared rules. Otherwise, it falls apart."

Ginger gave her a sideways look. "Do you feel like you and River have that?"

A knot, deep in the pit of her stomach formed from hearing her husband's name on her friend's lips. She exhaled slowly. "That's... the hard part. But yeah, I think we do."

"Kind of surprising, considering he comes off like a controlling, judgmental ass."

Tamar let out an inner sigh of relief. Ginger sure didn't sound any different towards him than she always did. Arnaq had to be wrong. "Sometimes people don't realize how they come off, they just need someone to be patient and willing to help them learn. River's brilliant, but he doesn't always realize how he sounds. In his head, he's defending what's right. Being real. To everyone else?" She shrugged. "Not so nice."

Ginger tilted her head. "And what was he when he

blackmailed me into cleaning toilets?"

Tamar smirked. "Oh, full on jerk. No defending that one."

They both laughed.

The conversation tapered off. Ginger's brow pinched slightly, eyes unfocused, tracking Tara as she crossed the camp. "Remember when Komi hit her?" she said, voice lower now. "All the women ganged up on him. Told him if he didn't stop, he could take his chances alone in the wilderness."

Tamar nodded, biting her bottom lip. "River was the only man there, wasn't he?"

"Yeah, but not because the others disagreed. They just figured it was a woman's issue. Some even got offended that he stepped in, like he was saying we couldn't handle it ourselves."

"That's not how he saw it. He thought he was standing with Tara."

Ginger studied her, needle paused mid-stitch. "Well... it worked. Komi's been solid since."

"Must have scared him straight."

"There just has to be accountability," Ginger said, returning to her thread. "Men didn't have that in the old world. Not really."

"Nobody did… but we had chocolate."

"And coffee. And pizza."

"And hamburgers. Ice cream. Streaming movies."

"And motors. Gears. Batteries."

"And botany labs. Every seed or plant I could get my hands on."

They fell quiet, staring at each other—grieving the excess, the noise, the ease.

Now they had sewing. And making babies.

And a world that no longer asked what they wanted. Just what they could survive.

A commotion on the north side of the village drew Tamar's attention.

Ginger rolled her eyes. "Probably that polar bear again."

The women grabbed their bows and ran toward the noise. Eight of them formed a loose half-circle, weapons raised, facing the massive white bear that had wandered too close. A female, by the look of her, thin, hungry. Probably out searching for food for her cubs.

They whooped and snarled, stomping the snow, sending a clear message: not today.

The bear hesitated, head low, then slowly turned and began to retreat.

"Notice how the men didn't even bother getting up," Ginger muttered to the group.

A few of the hunters—those who'd opted out of River's expedition—glanced over from their comfy pallets. Arms behind their head, feet luxuriously propped up.

Takumi gave a lazy wave. "Looked like you had it handled."

Ginger crossed her arms. "Hard to tell sometimes where support ends and plain old laziness begins."

"All right, all right," Takumi said, getting to his feet. He grabbed a spear, gave a cocky little hop, and flung it hard.

It sliced through the air—and hit.

The spear drove into the bear's throat.

The men cheered. "Nice shot," Dex congratulated.

Ginger's hands flew to her mouth, then she gritted her teeth at them. "Why would you do that?"

Takumi raised both hands like he was innocent. "What? Now we've got dinner. And I didn't even break a sweat."

Dex shook his head with a grin. "Typical. Ask for help, then complain when you get it."

"If you call that helping," Ginger snapped. "It was just a mother looking for food for her cubs. Now they're going to starve."

"Fewer bears does not sound like a bad thing, but of course you're not out there like we are," Dex added, shaking his head in judgement.

Takumi dropped back into his fur palette on the ground. The guys fist-bumped, laughing like it was a game.

Ginger didn't laugh. She crossed her arms tighter. "Is it just me, or are women's rights evaporating one hunt at a time?"

Tamar said nothing. Just shook her head and picked up her furs, walking home.

"Now how about you ladies go gut that bear?" Dex called from behind with a laugh.

"We're *all* supposed to do that," Ginger snapped.

Once inside, Tamar sifted through her pile of furs, flipping through the skins. She needed a tanned caribou hide for the next repair, and she knew she had at least one ready to go.

The door opened without a knock—normal here, but still made her shoulders stiffen. Takumi stepped in.

She didn't stop sorting, just saw him with a quick glance. "Need something?"

"Mind if we talk?"

"I'm right here." Her chest tightened, but she tried to not show it.

Takumi rubbed the back of his neck. "About the other day... I didn't mean to make you uncomfortable."

Tamar kept her eyes on the hides. "It's fine. I wasn't in a great mood. Sorry I snapped."

"I get it. You've got a lot on your plate. And now River's off on this... whatever-it-is."

She didn't respond. She found the hide she wanted to use, but decided to pretend busyness.

"Feels like this is the first time we've talked without *him* glaring at me."

She snorted. "Probably is."

An uncomfortable pause.

"Has Kallik said anything to River about... you know. Leadership changes?"

She looked up. "Why would he?"

"I've just noticed them talking more. That's all."

"River's just worried about him, making sure he's healing

up."

"Right." Takumi's voice flattened. "Except it doesn't look like that."

Tamar stopped what she was doing and rose to meet his gaze. "You're not going to use me to spy on my husband, Takumi."

"I would never use you…" He took an aggressive step forward, knocking a clay pot over. "You have to know that." His eyes searched her.

Her throat tightened. She stepped back without meaning to. Something in his voice had changed—too soft. Too close. There was more in Takumi's words than what he was actually saying.

"I should check on the kids," she muttered, moving for the door, desperate for escape.

He moved over, stepped into her path. Blocking it. Close enough that she felt it. She tried hard to keep her breathing in line.

"I may not want him as Pack Leader," he said, voice low. "But when we're out there—I keep him safe. He doesn't know it, but I do. For you. And for Heilo."

She met his eyes, steady. His breathing noticeably heavy.

"Thank you, Takumi," she said before stepping around him and slipped out the door, spine stiff, heart racing. Getting as far away from him as she could safely get.

She told herself he didn't mean it that way.

She told herself twice.

❧❄☙

Later that evening, River stepped inside their home. She flung her arms around his chest and arms.

He was stiff, not hugging her back. But she didn't care. She needed to feel his warmth on her. Something to undo the unease still crawling under her skin.

She needed this. Needed *him*—solid and real and hers.

"Did you kill it?" she whispered.

He was clean and his clothes were slightly damp. They must have bathed before coming home. Knowing her husband, it was some type of precaution.

“We did,” he said, something in his tone folding in on itself.

Tamar pulled back just enough to see his face. That wasn't the voice of a man returning from victory. “That’s good, right? It was dangerous?”

River didn’t look up. “No. It was just… wrong.” He eased past her to sit on his bed.

Silence hit and she stood there, trying to figure him out.

“Some things don’t belong in this world,” he said, voice low. “That doesn’t make them monsters.”

She brought her hands to her chest. “Did something happen?”

“I don’t want to talk about it.” He shook his head and got up to walk out, shoulders low, jaw set. She was left in their home, holding the weight of his silence.

❄

Tamar brought River a hollowed caribou horn of heated bone broth and settled beside him by the central fire. The evening air bit sharper than usual. Most of the community huddled close, wrapped in furs, except for a few teenage boys tearing through the snow shirtless in hide pants, shouting and laughing like the cold couldn’t touch them.

Two of them dropped onto the bare cold ground for a game of stick pull—legs braced together, both gripping a wooden rod. The goal was to lift the other off the ground or make them let go. So far, Heilo was undefeated among the younger kids and some of the teens as well.

"They're rowdier than usual," Tamar said, settling beside her husband and watching the chaos unfold as they battled it out for the next turn. "What exactly do they think that game will prove?"

"That they're ready to hunt," River replied, eyes fixed on the boys. "I'm watching. And they know it—especially Ukito."

A small grin tugged at Tamar's mouth. He was easing into his role, finally owning it.

"Yes, Ukito's grown strong," she said, attempting to join in with his critiques of a boy that they all watched grow up right before their eyes. Seemed like it was only a couple days ago he was eight, the age when they came back to earth. "He would be a fine addition."

Carson crawled behind them in a low crouch, glancing over his shoulder like a hunted animal.

"Carson, what are you doing?" Tamar asked, already suspicious.

"Shhh!" he hissed, wild-eyed. "Hiding."

"From who?" she whispered back, matching his tone.

"Kodik's sister."

"Hitty?" Tamar glanced at River.

River bent low with one eyebrow up and a sharp exhale. "Why?"

"Because that piece of caraboo-doo doo told her I have a crush on her!" Carson whispered furiously.

A loud voice cut through the crowd. "Carson!"

Hitty barreled into view, broad-shouldered and fast, shoving people aside like she was clearing brush. Carson squeaked and scrambled forward on all fours.

"Carson! Stop running from me!" Hitty shouted. "You come here!"

She lunged through a gap between two elders. Carson yelped and started hopping over people like a deranged hare.

Tamar shook her head. "What do you think she'll do if she catches him?"

River's eyebrow shot up, and a sly grin spread across his face. "Remember her pet squirrel?"

Tamar winced. "Run, Carson. Run!"

Cheering erupted as Harkin was helped to the central fire, flanked by two hunters and steadied by Kaya. He still limped and colored pale, but it was clear—he was going to make it.

"Ask him to sit near us," Tamar said, excited.

"He'll probably want to be alone with his wife and kid," River murmured.

"*Ask him.*"

River sighed and lifted a hand in invitation. "Sit with us tonight."

Harkin smiled at the gesture, carefully weaving past the others to settle beside them. Kaya eased him down, then tucked in at his side.

"So glad to see you up," Tamar said, leaning forward to speak around River, who leaned back, out in annoyance. "Kaya, what a nightmare."

"It was," Kaya admitted, squeezing Harkin's arm. "But he's strong."

"And everyone's been helpful of course."

"Oh, everyone's been wonderful. The baby's been passed between laps so I could stay with him, and the women have taken turns making soup for me to feed him. I've barely had to lift a finger."

Duncan stood and raised his hands to quiet the crowd. The murmurs faded as he launched into a dramatic retelling of an old-world fantasy tale of a ring with powers. His voice shifting with each character, the fire casting shadows that danced like living memories.

Heilo darted forward and plopped down beside River's legs, eyes wide with anticipation. "Oh! This is my favorite one."

But then Takumi stood.

The crowd stilled. Duncan froze mid-sentence. His eyes

slid to River.

"Forgive me, Duncan. I hate to interrupt you're amazing tale, but an outrageous act has occurred," Takumi's voice cut clean through the campfire hush.

Goosebumps prickled up Tamar's arms. *What was he doing?*

"One that demands attention," Takumi went on, stepping into the firelight. "River, acting as temporary Pack Leader under Kallik, led a hunt... and returned empty-handed. From what I've gathered, there was no reason for this. No urgency. No threat. No justification."

He shook his head, firelight catching in his eyes. "We don't waste life. We don't hunt for pride. But this outsider—" He pointed to River, slow and deliberate "—thinks he can lead our community and spit on our ways. And now, with whispers that he may be made Pack Leader, I have no choice but to challenge him."

Tamar's gut twisted. Challenge how? In a fight, River would flatten him, no question. What was Takumi thinking?

Kallik rose slowly. "I will remind you all, that there are *no outsiders*. I don't want to ever hear such talk." He glared at Takumi. "Unity isn't just important, it's *survival*. Division cannot fester. But it is festering and growing. One side for Takumi, the other for River. This must be dealt with and it must be dealt with in the right way. The elders have remembered an old way that may help us and at Takumi's request—it will be used." He glanced between the two men. "A song duel. Winner becomes Pack Leader."

"Oh cool. Like a rap battle," Carson said, nodding eagerly between them. Guess he got away from Hitty.

"I don't sing," River said flatly.

"Well, you're going to have to," Kallik replied.

"I don't *sing*," River snapped again, more force this time.

Takumi smirked. That was the plan. He knew exactly what he was doing, and he knew his enemy well.

"Then Takumi wins," Kallik announced, lifting a hand.

Carson immediately shot to his feet, waving his hand. "I'll do it! Let me do it for him!"

"You will perform on River's behalf?"

Carson nodded his head in excess, jogging in place. Kallik bent to confer with the elders.

Takumi's face darkened. "That's not how this works," he snapped. "If River forfeits, he forfeits. He has to speak for himself."

Carson bounced higher. "Please, please, come on!"

Kallik straightened. "The Elders were looking forward to some entertainment, so let's give it to them—Carson may speak for River."

"Oh my gosh," River groaned, dragging a hand down his face. "I'm going to regret this."

Carson and Takumi stepped into the circle forming of spectators around them. River stood behind Carson, arms crossed, eyes locked on his challenger.

Kallik raised both hands. "Since he's being challenged, River goes first."

Carson tapped his mouth with his front knuckle, like he was thinking, as the low drum beats boom.

He pointed at Takumi. "*You're farts smell like raw meat.*"

Takumi snickered, with a glance back at his group.

"*When it lingers—it's a dead fish between your butt cheeks.*"

Takumi laughed harder with a snort, grabbing his knees.

Carson closed the gap between them, arms wide.

"You act big now, but you're soft inside,
Riding River's shadow like it's a free ride.
It's dogs, dogs, dogs—your one-track life.
Did they wag their tails better than your wife?"

Takumi shakes his head to Arnaq while putting his hands to

his heart. She blows a kiss at him.

"Your family ran a dog-sled tourist trap.
That's not legacy, so cut the crap.
Sucking up to millionaires, you did that a lot.
Which is weird—because you hate the one rich boy we got."

"You can't keep pace with him—
His excellence a festering-wound-on-your-ego, filled to the brim.
You envy his son. You envy his name.
Kallik picked him—so get over your shame."

"Every winter, he hauls more fish and seal than you.
As a hunter, you will never beat him, I argue.
'Cause you're stuck in your old glory days of dog tours
And what's worse... his woman's better than yours."

A collective groan went out among the coward.

Arnaq held her hands out in disbelief, "How? She can't sew!"

Tamar shook her head at Carson, cutting the air with her hand. "Leave us out of this."

Takumi's turn. He rubbed his hands together while pursing his lips, glaring right at River as Carson sat down,

"You know... it's not surprising...
You had someone else do this for you—can't you guys see?
And this is who you want your new Pack leader to be?
You're pig-headed, cocky, petty, and rude.
We are all so sick of dealing with your bad moods"

.

"Such a prissy pose boy, you're afraid of germs
I love eating raw meat and watching you squirm

You're touchy, sensitive, such a delicate little bell.

If you had it your way, the whole camp would walk on egg shells."

A loathsome person, I can't help that that's true.

So much, so, that your own mother left you.

You think you're so great, but where have you been?

Your wive's so lonely, she has to talk to OTHER MEN."

River lunged forward and punched Takumi clean in the face. Takumi reeled but rallied fast, charging at him like a bull.

River caught the momentum, twisted, and flung him, slamming him to the ground.

Dust sprayed in the firelight.

The crowd surged backward in disbelief.

Arnaq shrieked and charged, elbow raised to hammer River's back.

Tamar didn't think—she moved. If Arnaq joined, so did she.

She slammed her shoulder into the woman's ribs. Arnaq stumbled and went down hard.

"Tamar!" Arnaq gasped, shock in her voice.

River and Takumi rolled in the dirt, grappling for dominance. Takumi kicked free, and River scrambled upright, just as Tamar pressed her back to his.

They moved together without speaking, instinct snapping into place. Same stance. Same rhythm.

River glanced over his shoulder, breathless. His eyes caught hers—surprise flickering there, edged with something like awe.

Not for the fight.

For her.

Takumi lunged again. River backhanding him clean across the cheek.

Tamar spun to meet Arnaq's second charge—But Dex came barreling in from River's blind side.

Tamar kicked Arnaq backward, then pivoted, her leg whipping up in a perfect roundhouse that cracked across Dex's jaw. He went down hard.

River tore his arm free from Takumi's grip and snap-kicked him in the ribs—just as Tamar's leg struck from the other side. Takumi crumpled with a guttural groan, landing flat on his rear.

River and Tamar landed side by side, feet hitting the dirt in near unison. They shared a quick glance, shared breath, same fight.

"That is enough!" Kallik's voice cracked across the fire circle. "Unity is precious. Do you not understand this?"

"Unity? With *him*?" Takumi staggered back up, holding his ribs. "He's the one who threw the first punch." He jabbed a finger at River. "This is what you call leadership?"

Tamar leaned in toward River, voice low. "Trip him."

"What?" River's eyebrow went up as Takumi continued to rail against him.

"Get him on the ground again. *Now.*"

River didn't hesitate, but grabbed Takumi from behind and hooked his leg. Takumi hit the ground hard, the air huffing out of him. He scrambled up, wincing.

"Again!" Tamar bit, not caring who heard.

River tripped him again, then stood over him, fists clenched. "How can you lead, Takumi, if you can't even stand up?"

Takumi didn't answer. He looked past River—straight at Tamar, hurt in his eyes.

Dex, Upa, Kota, and the others surged forward, ready to pounce. But Big John stepped in, blocking their path. Tamar with him, forcing them back.

Kodiak moved to stand beside Big John. Then Carson did. Then Ginger and Noah. Duncan. Osha. Sura. Jason. Even Harkin hobbled forward, Kaya bracing him as he stood tall.

All these people—on their side?

River glanced around, face in disbelief of what was behind

him.

He learned it. She could see that he had finally learned it.

It was her turn to teach him something. Real power was not in raw strength, but in numbers, and you can't have numbers without friends.

Kallik stepped forward. "The elders have decided. River, you will be the new Pack Leader. Takumi—your choice is to accept, or leave."

All eyes were now on Takumi.

He could leave. Start his own community. Break them in two.

Tamar met his eyes. She begged him not to, without words.

Takumi straightened, and held River's gaze. "I accept," he said, lip curled like it cost him.

Kallik let out a breath. One Tamar hadn't realized she too, was holding.

"Hurray! Now let's all go relax and listen to this great story," Kallik called, arms lifted as he herded the group back toward the fire.

The crowd drifted toward Duncan's pit. Osha scooped up Bly and took Heilo by the hand, settling down in front of her husband.

But Tamar didn't move.

She stayed behind, heart aching at the uncertain look on River's face. The fire blazed behind him. The rest of the community faded into the distance.

He stood in front of her, chest still heaving. "I didn't think you were on my side anymore."

The words landed sharp and unexpected. Not as an accusation, but a wound.

Tamar blinked. "What would ever make you think that?"

River went still. His lips pressed tight, and his eyes dropped to the ground.

Tamar's stomach twisted. This wasn't about pants.

It wasn't even about the title.

This was deeper.

The kind of hurt that didn't yell. The kind that just stood there, quiet, cracking everything you built apart.

"Before my birthday…" River's voice thinned. He sniffed once, wiped his chin like it might buy him time. "I heard you—talking to Takumi."

Her breath caught. She covered her mouth and knees buckled as the memory slammed back.

"You were apologizing to him," River went on, voice tight. "Said I was difficult."

Her chest tightened so hard she thought it would burst.

"And then you said—" his voice faltered. "—at least you don't have to be married to him.'"

The silence hung as he waited for her to speak. She held herself, not sure what else to do. "You heard that?"

He nodded, slow and heavy, the ache plain across his face.

What had she done?

She'd said it on impulse. Forgotten it the moment it passed. She had no idea he'd been nearby.

"River… I'm so sorry." Her voice cracked. "I shouldn't have said that."

He didn't look at her. His hand dropped limp at his side. "You're only sorry now because you know I heard."

"That's not true." She stepped toward him, hand resting lightly on his chest. "It wasn't true. I'm telling you—"

"*Tamar*," he snapped.

She froze.

His eyes were wide. Crestfallen. "You wouldn't have said it... if it wasn't."

She tried to remember how she'd felt that day. The frustration. The exhaustion. Feelings she didn't even recognize anymore.

She shook her head. "You're wrong." She held her hands out to him. "I said it out of emotion. Not what I really felt."

"Well then how am I supposed to know what's real?"

"Ask," she said, "And give me time to answer."

He laughed, but it was hollow. "Then it's not real. You're just saying what you know you should."

Her eyes narrowed. "Even if it is—what's so wrong with that? Saying the right thing, even when it's hard? Doesn't that show commitment?" She bit her bottom lip. "Isn't that love at its highest form?"

"I don't want to be together if it's because you think you have to be. I grabbed your hand. I called you my wife. You had no choice in it."

"I had every choice in it! You think I'm so stupid I can't say no?"

"There is nothing stupid about you."

"You haven't been treating me like you believe that."

"Guess it's my turn to apologize."

"I don't need an apology, when I still haven't received forgiveness."

He took a deep breath and glanced away. His expression shifted. Resolute now.

"I need to say something, and I need you not to interrupt me. Let me get it all out."

She nodded. Her heart pounded in her ears. Was this going to be bad... or good? Was he going to tell her they can't be together anymore?

"I was never under any delusion that I could hold onto you," he said. "But I hoped. I really hoped. And if you'd rather be with someone else... I won't stop you. So do whatever you need to do. But make your decision now. I can't do this back and forth anymore." His eyes showed his pain.

Laughter struck in the background from the story, but they both held their gaze on one another.

"Can I speak now?"

He nodded.

She stepped closer, right in his face. Her eyes narrowed. "And just who do you think I'd be happier with?"

He didn't answer. Just breathed.

"I swear, if you say *Takumi,* I will slap you in the face."

He stepped back, sighed with his shoulders slumped. "I'm giving you an out."

"I didn't ask for your out."

They stared at each other again, and she bit her bottom lip. "So wait? All this time, you've been trying to push me away?"

He glanced off in the distance. "I thought…maybe you needed a nudge."

Anger boiled in her chest. "What kind of husband pushes his wife toward her own destruction? Leaves her starving for affection?"

"I just want you to be happy," River said quietly. "Even if it's not with me."

"Then *let* me be happy!"

He glanced up, startled. Eyes wide.

She pressed a hand to her chest. "You don't let me be. You're always watching, waiting to point out what's wrong. Always ready to correct or criticize. I'm already hard enough on myself, River—I don't need your voice echoing mine. I don't need you making it harder to love you."

He hesitated. "I can't help seeing the cracks," he murmured. "And once I see them, I can't unsee them. That's not about you. That's just... my head."

He turned toward the moonlight, its reflection rippling across the water. "Sometimes," he said, "I feel this darkness inside me. When I get emotional, it wants to erupt. I'm doing everything I can to hold it in. But I'm scared, Tamar. Scared I won't be able to contain it."

The boiling in her gut went still.

He didn't look grieved. He looked terrified—like he was bracing for her to leave the second she saw it. *Is that why he was really pushing her away?*

If it was, then he needed the exact opposite.

Not caring how he reacted, she threw her arms around him.

Startled at first, he sighed into her shoulder and held her tight.

The poor man had no idea how to carry feelings outside a box. Of course they terrified him.

She squeezed his hand. “I’m not afraid of your darkness. Whatever you’re going through,” she whispered, “We go through it together. So you’re stuck with me.” She gave him a crooked grin.

His voice was quiet. “Then why would you say that to him? About me?”

“I shouldn’t have,” she said. “It was wrong. I was angry… and it came out sideways.”

“Angry about what?”

She looked away. “You’re just… so unaffectionate. And I —”

A breath caught in her chest. “Sometimes I want to be held so badly it hurts.”

“I hug you every time you ask.”

“But that’s just it. I have to ask.”

River nodded slowly. “It doesn’t come naturally to me.”

She studied him, voice soft but frayed. “A squeeze on the shoulder. A gentle touch. Holding my hand. I need those things. How is that not natural?”

He looked down. “I don’t know how to answer that.” His jaw tightened. A muscle ticked near his temple. His hands flexed once at his sides, then stilled, as if even that much movement gave too much away. “The more I let myself feel…” His voice lowered, rougher now. “…the more control you’ll have over me.”

“You think I’m trying to control you?”

“Of course you are. It’s what all human beings do. Every interaction is about control.”

She stared at him, trying to absorb what he’d just said. “You’re so afraid of being controlled,” she murmured, “that you’re the one doing the controlling.”

"Maybe."

"No *maybe* about it." She hesitated, chewing the edge of her lip. "Sometimes I get so angry. I feel... tricked. You were affectionate when we were dating." Her voice caught. "Then I married you, and it was like a switch flipped. Is that what men do? Offer warmth to win someone over, then pull it back once she can't leave?"

He flinched—barely. But she caught it.

"Is that what women do?" he said, voice low. "Say they love you, then run to your rival and tell him what a pain you are?" His gaze fell, thumb scraping against his palm like he needed something to grip. "I didn't trick you. I just didn't realize I was changing. Not until life got real."

Her expression softened. "Marriage is hard."

"Marriage is hard," he echoed, quieter now.

"Did we rush into it? Were we too young?"

"As if people in their thirties and forties don't screw it up too," he said, mouth twitching. "But yeah… maybe we have less wisdom. Less perspective. Still wouldn't have waited. I was ready for my life to start with you."

"I feel the same," she murmured, thumb picking at the collar seam on her parka.

"You know, the day I was born has never felt worth celebrating," he said, voice low. "But there's one day that is. The day we met. Really met."

"In the gym?" she said quietly, brows lifting.

He nodded. "I've marked it every year since. That's when my life really started." He shifted, tucking a few loose strands of hair behind his ear. "That's when I finally had a reason to wake up in the morning."

Her lips pressed together in thought. It had never even crossed her mind to mark the day. "Why didn't you tell me?" she whispered. "We could have celebrated it together."

He shrugged. "You never brought it up. I figured, maybe it didn't matter to you."

Pain pitched in her chest, pulling it tight. He'd carried that so quietly, for so long. All that devotion, tucked away like it didn't deserve space. "Then let's celebrate it," she said, voice low. "Every year. Together." She tilted her head. "What do you do?

"I take the dried primrose blossoms," he said, "and toss them into the water. Just—watch them spin. And replay that day in my head so I never lose it."

"That sounds beautiful." She stepped in, slow and sure, and wrapped her arms around him.

He let out a breath against her hair, then rested his head on hers, squeezing her back like he meant it. "Neshama sheli," he whispered. *My soul.* The words sent tingles down her arms and up the back of her neck. A Hebrew name she'd taught him, the one he only used when she meant *everything.*

He leaned down and kissed her cheek, his voice quieter now, almost reverent. "You're really here, aren't you?

She pulled back just enough to see him. His face was so close, every freckle and shadow etched by the firelight. For a heartbeat, she just breathed him in—the familiar scent of spiced wood mixed with fresh artic air, the warmth of his breath against her skin, the sharp rush of disbelief—and then she cupped his face and pressed her lips to his.

No words, just an answer.

Then again. And again. Harder.

Her fingers slid behind his neck, pulling him closer, until there was no space left between them at all. She barely breathed the words. "You know... it's dark enough. We could sneak back to our home while everyone's distracted."

His breath caught. "If you're suggesting what I think you're suggesting... that's cruel," he whispered. "Cruel to get me that excited."

She bit her bottom lip, eyes gleaming with mischief. "Come on." A giggle slipped out, as she scrunched her nose and tugged his hand.

He shook his head, sharp and fast, and leaning back like he didn't dare believe it. "This better not be a trick."

"Shhh." She pressed a finger to her lips with a giggle, nearly to the door.

They stumbled into their home, with subconscious giggles and awkward moments like they were virgins again and it was their first time. Tripping over boots and tangled limbs, they collapsing onto the white fur rug with a thud. Knocking the breath out of him which brought her to a quiet, hard laughter.

"You think that's funny, do you?" he said, rough and amused before she kissed him again. He pressed her into him with his strength, kissing her back with a tender lower lip while his hand weaved into her hair, gripping it.

She felt his muscular arms until he rolled her underneath him, warm, solid and real.

He kissed her like a man starved, urgent and aching, lips soft but steady as he poured every unspoken word, every bottled-up moment, melting into her.

Oh, how she'd missed that. The solid press of his chest, his rough skin against her cheek, the mingled taste of salty and sweet on his lips. Heat unfurled inside her, sharp and dizzying, until she didn't know where her body ended and his began.

She needed him close, needed to tear off his parka and feel the familiar strength of his hunter's chest beneath her hands. She needed skin on skin.

To be seen again. Touched again. Known.

Loved.

The ache bloomed deep, sharp enough to steal her breath as a moan escaped from his mouth. He kissed behind her ear, tracing down her neck to her breastbone. Then he paused, hovering, gaze drinking her in like he was trying to memorize every inch. His brow arched, trembling with wonder.

Holding back. Making her wait.

She scoffed, impatience laughing through the ache. "Oh *come on!* Get this parka off me already."

His mouth curved against her throat, a half-smile, half-growl. “Bossy,” he said, voice low and dangerous. “Only you get to talk to me like that.”

Her pulse kicked, a thrill shooting through her with one eyebrow up. “Let’s keep it that way,” she whispered, tugging his top off, over his head.

His gaze caught hers for half a second—hot, dark, almost feral—before his mouth claimed hers again. His breath ghosted over her ear, rough and ragged. “I am *so* going to ravage you, with everything I’ve held back these last few months.”

She met his gaze, excitement lit her face, a glint of heat and challenge in her eyes. “That sounds like a promise.”

His answering kiss left no room for doubt. Heat, fierce and unrelenting, curled between them with hands tangled and breath quickened.

He gathered her close, holding her as though he could shield her from every shadow, and every storm. And then there was nothing but the blur of wanting and finding, their heavy fur clothing tangling and falling away, until the world beyond their walls ceased to exist and satisfaction took hold.

And the two once again became one. Physically, emotionally… spiritually.

For the first time in too long, the distance between them shattered, spilling light into every dark, aching place they’d been carrying alone. And in that fragile, perfect space, they could once again feel safe in each other’s arms.

In a moment only about the both of them, she laid on his bare chest, listening to his heartbeat and the rise and fall of his breathing as he caressing her bare shoulder and back with his gentle fingers.

No need to speak. No more words to say.

The moonlight beat on the wall of their canvas hut, the commotion outside long dissipated and gone.

He lifted her hand, fiddling with the Sarcosa ring that never left her finger. With a raised eyebrow, he brought the hand to his lips and kissed it with a firm hold of his lips, then kissed the top of her head, his arms squeezing her tight, breathing her in deep, as she drifted off to sleep to the rhythm of his heart and breath.

Nine

TAMAR ROSE EARLY, before the sun had done more than skim the snowbanks with light. She packed River's gear, then took the pot outside to scoop fresh snow for breakfast tea. Bly and Heilo were already out, playing as usual, bundled and shrieking in the cold.

Behind her, Carson's voice called out. "Well, somebody had a good night last night."

She didn't turn to look at him. "Mind your own business, Carson."

"If I can hear it, it's my business." Carson stood nearby, pipe in hand, watching the kids kick up powder. The snow fresh and soft from the night's flurries. "So we're back to that again. I think I liked it better when you two hated each other. I think the whole camp liked it better."

"We never hated each other—"

Hitty stomped in a rampage towards Tamar. She marched right up to her, shaking her fist. "Where's that good-for-nothing man of yours?"

Tamar straightened, bristling. "Excuse me?"

"I know he took it! He was eyeing it all last night."

Tamar blinked, then turned to call out to Carson. "She doing that thing where she accuses everyone again?"

Carson took a puff of his pipe. "You know it."

Tamar sighed "Just what are you talking about, Hitty?"

"My knife, of course! Don't play dumb. Where is he?"

"Preparing to risk his life so you can have something to eat," Tamar snapped. "And he didn't take your knife." She was with him all night.

Before Hitty could respond, a shrill shriek split the air. Kodik burst out of his canvas tent wearing nothing but underwear, bald as a newborn—eyebrows and beard gone. He flailed at his head like it was on fire. "Car-son!" he wailed. "What have you done?!"

Carson was already twirling Hitty's beautifully carved whale bone knife above his head like a trophy. "Run, kids! It's an *idukupa!*"

The children screamed and scattered, chasing after Carson as he darted across the snow, howling like a banshee.

Heads poked out of their canvas tents as the commotion grew. Those watching saw the bald Kodik and burst into laughter.

"Somebody drank too much last night," Nukilik called out, laughing off to the side with Upa.

Kodik ignored him, stumbling barefoot through snowdrifts in pursuit of Carson. Who was terrifying the kids more than leading them.

Tamar folded her arms and turned back to Hitty, with one eyebrow up. Hitty just glared for a beat, then huffed, and charged after Carson.

River poked his head out of their home, shirtless and eyes squinting against the brightness. "What is going on?"

Tamar answered with one word. "Carson."

River exhaled through his nose, rolled his eyes and retreated back inside.

❧❄☙

It had been three days. No sign of the hunting team.

He had left, and she felt it in her body. An ache, raw and heavy, like the echo of his touch. A physical reminder that he wasn't with her. The burn in his eyes as he turned to leave with the awaiting hunting team had showed he felt the very same.

Seemed cruel to split them up like this, after they just got back together.

Tamar kept her hands busy—mending clothes, stitching parkas, teaching the kids their reading and letters—anything to keep the fear at bay. She'd lee cold through an open flap.

The day was bright, a kinarned long ago: let your mind idle, and the worry creeps in like thd of sharp Arctic sunlight that glittered off the snow and made it twinkle. A steady brisk wind rolled through camp.

Osha sat beside her, a sewing bundle in her lap, hands working a steady rhythm.

"Beautiful day," Tamar said quietly.

"Yes," the older woman agreed, not looking up. "Very beautiful. Enjoy. It'll be the last for a while."

Tamar paused. "You're sure?"

Osha nodded, steady as ever. "Winter storm will be here by evening."

Tamar didn't question it. The elders always seemed to know before the sky did. A shift in the wind, the scent in the air. They didn't need clouds to read what was coming.

Very soon, it will be time to hunker down in the igluit for the long winter. They would trudge to the winter location, cut huge ice bricks, and connect many small igloos to one large common space, locking them all inside for three months.

It was a time of community, fun games, drum dancing, and rest. And everyone will definitely be on each other's nerves by the end.

She glanced toward the horizon. Still nothing. Just snow, low light and too much space.

River, where are you?

Heilo snatched Bly's hide scrape doll, and she dropped to the ground in a full-body tantrum.

"Heilo! Give it back!" Tamar snapped, hanging coats on the drying sticks staked into the snow.

Heilo tossed the doll to the ground beside her and crossed his arms in a pout. The expression was pure River.

Tamar sighed, walked over, picked up the doll, and handed it back to him. "Not like that. You know better. What do you even want with a doll?"

"I was just looking at it," he muttered. "The arm looked broken. She didn't have to act like that."

"What you did wasn't kind. Now hand it back—*nicely*—and say you're sorry."

He obeyed, grumbling but compliant. Oh he was going to be such a handful once he was a teenager. She could already see it.

She watched them for a second—two little humans absorbing everything around them and returning it in sparks and shouts.

There was a certain wonder that came with motherhood. A wonder she had sometimes forgotten.

Thoughts of her father came. A part of her knew it wasn't realistic, but she still hoped he was alive somewhere. That's what she told herself. That he had somehow survived. And someday he'd find her.

Her sister's picture still hung by her bed, and her kids knew her as "*Aunt Kacey*". If only she had a physical picture of him too.

She just had her Pharos…that will run out of power soon. 12% left.

12% she was saving but would degrade whether she used it or not.

Jason sprinted to her, kicking snow. "Nurse Laney needs you right now. It's about Harkin."

"I thought he was doing better?"

Jason just shook his head. “Don’t know. She said to come get you, and fast.”

Tamar turned to Osha. “Can you watch the kids?”

The old woman nodded, already moving closer. Tamar hustled to the clinic.

Inside, Harkin lay on the wooden table, shivering from the blocks of packed ice surrounding him. Aisha, Laney’s assistant, was frantically pressing more around his leg. It melted quickly into dripping puddles on the ground.

“Thank the stars you’re here,” Nurse Laney said, not looking up. “He’s relapsed. I need Usnea—and I need it fast.”

Tamar’s chest tightened. “But the tincture will take at least twenty-four hours to make!”

“Exactly why I need the lichen *now.*” Laney snapped the words as she checked his temperature with the camp’s only surviving thermometer. “I’m taking the leg.”

Tamar slapped her hands to her cheeks. “But—Kaya—”

“I don’t care anymore.” Laney’s eyes flared. “Harkin matters to us too. We’re Moon Crew. We get a say. The elders can scold me later.”

But…that was not what they all agreed to.

Tamar stood frozen as Laney tightened the tourniquet. Aisha was sharpening the long metal saw with fast, focused strokes.

Is this really happening? Harkin was going to lose his leg?

“Tamar!” Laney barked, snapping her out of it. “Get it. Now.”

With urgency in her step, Tamar rushed from the clinic, then slowed as she neared her home. Her pace down to a crawl.

Should she tell Laney? About River? About how he didn’t want her leaving without him?

No. That wasn’t Laney’s burden. Whatever fallout came—this was Tamar’s choice to make.

She turned and ran. “Jason!” she called, catching sight of him near his drying racks. “Remember last year, when you helped me find Usnea lichen?"

He blinked at her. "Uh, yeah. I think so?"

"Do you think you could find it again?"

"Maybe." He scratched the back of his neck. "It's the one that grows kind of stringy, right?"

Tamar's heart sank.

"Jason… it's for Harkin. Life or death."

He froze. Said nothing.

Tamar sighed. Of course. He wouldn't be able to tell it apart from the other lichens. And it grew too far out, too deep into the cooler forest zones. If he guessed wrong, or took too long...

It would be too late.

She couldn't let that happen.

She *wouldn't.*

Which meant... she had to go.

Alone.

She stood still for a breath, bracing against the weight of what that meant. River was going to be furious. She'd just got him back. They'd just found their rhythm again—barely. And this would shatter it.

This would shatter his trust.

But love wasn't safety. It was risk. It was stepping into the cold when someone else needed you more.

And what if it were reversed? What if River was the one on that pallet? She'd beg Kaya to go. To *run.*

Her stomach knotted. *He's going to be so mad.*

So she wouldn't tell anyone this time. No chance of being called out, like last time.

She'd do what needed to be done and maybe she'd get back before him.

No explanations. No witnesses. No permission.

She found Duncan and asked if he and Osha could watch the kids for a few hours. He agreed—he always did.

Then she packed fast, slinging her satchel and knife belt over her shoulder.

Please watch over me, she whispered to God under her breath. And slipped into the snow without another word. Passed the snow banks along the lagoon, without anyone noticing.

❄

Three days of hard tracking, and finally—caribou sign.

But not many.

River knelt beside the prints. Shallow. Melt-softened. Fading fast.

They were behind the migration.

The herd was moving south, burrowing down or already gone. Winter was already here.

"I know you're tired," he called, voice low but firm. "We all are. But we don't have time. Pick it up."

The team pushed forward. Big John had spotted the tracks. Now they followed him, cutting through a long stretch of wind-crusted scrub toward the tree line.

There—between the spruce. A large buck, grazing alone.

River raised his hand to halt.

The wind was good, pushing their scent back. He motioned with two fingers: Big John, take half the crew, flank wide.

They moved in slow and quiet. It was a big one. Good meat, heavy with late-summer fat. A find like this could tip the whole camp's chances for the season.

River stayed back, crouched low behind a moss-slick rock.

The team did the work.

One arrow. Then Two. The animal dropped clean. No panic, no pain.

River exhaled. "Quick," he said. "Dress it here."

They slit it open fast, pulling organs aside, leaving the scent-rich entrails for the wolves.

"We're cutting through the trees," River decided. "It'll

shave off two days."

"Rough haul with a travois," Carson muttered, already shouldering a pole.

"We rotate more often. Six hands on the meat at all times. Two in front, Two in back, Two on the sides for stability." It was going to take some serious coordination, but they could do it. He knew they could.

The crew worked in rhythm, tying the carcass to the travois with a canvas and three cross bars. River took the lead, keeping the pace steady.

Then—Nukilik stopped.

River turned to him. "What is it?"

He didn't answer right away. Just sniffed the air. Tasted it.

Kodik joined him. "Blizzard."

River blinked. "You sure?"

Big John crouched and tapped the ground. "Pinecones are open. Wind's shifted. Feels like it's riding heavy."

River scanned the sky. The light had changed. Diffuse. Dim. Still no clouds—but the way the wind dragged across the trees...

It was coming.

"Move!" he barked. "Fast as you can."

They took off. No more rotating. No more pace. Just raw urgency now. Others grabbed the pole sides. Carson. Dex. Even Takumi.

River didn't look back.

Nukilik broke into a run, climbing the nearest hill, scanning the horizon.

River caught up with him at the top.

"What do you see?" he called, breath steaming.

Nukilik squinted north. "Not yet. But it's rolling in. Maybe an hour."

River's stomach dropped.

They needed three.

Carson groaned. "You think we can make it?"

"Depends on how fast your lazy hides can go." His leadership style was definitely not like Kallik's.

River ran back in front of the travois. "When you think you can take a side, rotate out. Can you keep with my pace?"

The men shout and whoop, eager to prove. They hauled as one now, driven, loud, and alive.

Snow crust cracked under their boots. Even the meat stayed attached to the travois, never flinging off.

Then River looked back.

Far on the horizon, just above the black tree line, the clouds began to build. Not fast. Not loud.

But curling.

Stacking.

The kind of stillness that came before something broke, before the world shifted sideways. It prickled across his skin, coiled tight in his gut.

He didn't speak. Just clenched the rope and moved faster.

Ten

THE WIND PICKED up, hard and sharp now, driving snow in fast horizontal lines. Storm clouds boiled at their heels, curling low, and dark.

No time left.

The hunting team broke into a full run, dragging the carcass the final stretch toward the village. They dropped the kill just outside the boundary—no sense hauling it farther. The cold would keep it.

River bolted for home.

So much to do. The oil skins had to be wrapped and brought in. The outer walls had to be checked for rips. They needed at least three days of food inside. Blankets ready. Heat banked.

He yanked open the hide flap.

Empty.

His gut clenched. Where was Tamar?

He ran back outside. Snow lashed his cheeks. Ice crust stung his lashes.

Duncan was out reinforcing his walls, tying the ropes tight. River caught his eye.

"The kids are inside," Duncan said, as if reading his mind.

"Where's Tamar?"

"She dropped them off after talking to Laney. I think she's

helping her with something."

River's feet moved before the words finished. Straight to the clinic.

He pushed through the canvas door—then froze.

That smell.

Faint copper. Raw meat and stillness.

Death.

A sheet draped a body on the slab table. Still. Fresh.

Harkin.

No. No, no, no.

He didn't need to turn to know Laney was behind him. Her footsteps were soft and hesitant.

"What happened?" River asked, voice low and rough.

"He went septic. Fast." Her voice trembled. "One minute he was joking with Kaya… then he spiked, threw up and went quiet. I couldn't stop it."

River stared at the sheet. At what was Harkin.

The storm outside howled louder, clawing at the seams of the clinic.

He wasn't ready for this. He wasn't ready for what it meant for the tribe.

Where was Tamar?

River finally turned to face her. Laney's eyes were rimmed red, her cheeks raw from wiping tears.

Guilt surged low in his gut. If only he'd sensed the bear sooner. Posted a better watch. Called it earlier.

"We'll have to look after Kaya," he said quietly.

Laney nodded, arms folded tight. "She's shattered. Time's all I've got for her now."

River gave a shallow nod. Let the silence sit for a breath. Then—

"Have you seen Tamar?"

Laney blinked. "My last effort to try to save him. She said she was taking Jason to look for Usnea, but…" Her eyes dropped. "They didn't make it back in time."

River's stomach flipped. His pulse lurched. He didn't wait for any more information, he spun and bolted out into the cold.

Laney's voice called after him, but he didn't stop.

He found Jason near the food racks, stripping meat from the earlier haul. Relief hit him like a hammer to the chest.

He placed a hand on his shoulder. "Jason! Oh thank goodness. Where's Tamar?"

Jason blinked, confused. "She's missing?"

"You—were supposed to be with her." River waved his hands in a frustrated and stiff motion. "When did you get back?"

"I never went anywhere," Jason said.

River's jaw clenched. "Okay, then when did you last *see* her?"

"Earlier today. She was explaining some plant Fitzgibbons needed. Usnea, I think. Then she…" Jason's eyes widened. "You don't think she went to get it alone, do you?"

River grabbed him by the coat, teeth grit. "And you let her?"

"I didn't know, man. I thought she was just prepping."

River let him go and took off. Straight to the tent. Grabbed his sword and hunting gear. Buckled the holster. Slipped the knife belt across his chest with hands that moved too fast.

Outside, the wind screamed down the ridge as he bore through it. Duncan spotted him from his shelter wall, walking towards the white. "Where are you going?"

River didn't pause. "To find Tamar." He was already past the last tent.

"You *can't* go out there now. A blizzard's coming!" Duncan's voice rose against the wind. He stepped in front of him. "You'll die if you leave."

River didn't blink. "So will she."

He tried to pass, but Duncan grabbed his arm. "Don't do it."

River yanked free, fire flashing in his eyes. "Back. Off."

Duncan didn't flinch. "Do you think she'd want you to

freeze to death? She's smart. If the storm caught her, she'll dig in. She knows what to do. But if *you* go out there now, looking for her—you won't survive it. And she'll come back to find you gone."

River got right in his face. "I'm not leaving her out there!"

Duncan grabbed him and tried to pull him back. "And I'm not going to let you kill yourself."

River reared his arm back and punched him in the face. Duncan staggered, then River took off in a run. Duncan ran after him, leaping out with outstretched hands and grabbed his leg. River fell to the ground. He tried to kick him off, but he also didn't want to seriously hurt him.

"Kick and punch me all you want. Break my bones. You're going to have to kill me before I let you do this. What would Tamar want you to do? Even if she's in trouble. Would she want you to leave your kids as orphans?"

"Stop it, Duncan!"

"You *will* freeze to death."

River stopped kicking. Tamar's voice echoed in his head, *"He's right, don't be stubborn."* He looked down at the ground. The wind picked up as the snow began to fall in a curtain.

The wind wailed. Snow peeled down in thick, slanting sheets. A curtain of white swallowing the world.

"Go take care of your children, the men will go out as soon as it's over and we will find her," Duncan shouts.

His face wrenched with pain. "I can't!"

"Yes, you can." He looked back at the storm. "You have no other choice."

Duncan let go of his legs and helped him up, leading him back. River didn't resist.

Together, they turned back toward the glow of his home, as the storm closed in.

Eleven

River paced Duncan's home, as a caged animal. Back and forth. Back and forth. His kids sitting quietly, watching him with concern in their eyes.

Osha had brought soup that her and Sura made—setting it quietly on the same table near him—but he didn't touch it. Didn't even glance at it. His eyes kept flicking to the door, every shift of wind making him the more restless.

"It could be days," Duncan said gently, hands out in appeal.

River didn't answer. Didn't stop moving.

"You need rest. You'll be no good to her if you drop out there."

Still pacing. But eventually, even he had limits.

After an hour, the storm pressed in so thick it blurred even the nearest shelter walls. The white was total. Unforgiving. Nipping at him.

You left her out in that. You monster.

Finally, River sat. Not by choice. Just… ran out of steam.

He slept like someone forced. Barely out, barely able to keep his eyes closed. Heilo and Bly right next to him, their warmth giving him an ounce of comfort. The night and half the day passed.

Then a nudge. "River. It's clearing," Duncan's voice rang.

His eyes snapped open. He didn't speak. Just moved.

Out the door. Into the cold.

"Wait!" Duncan shouted behind him.

He didn't stop.

Duncan chased after, snow already knee-high. He hurled the snowshoes Ginger had made for him two seasons back. River caught them mid-stride, gave a tight nod, and kept going.

He strapped them on while half-buried, legs already soaked through. The fit was awkward, the bindings stiff from cold. He stumbled upright, breath fogging, then pushed forward into the untouched white.

The wilderness was dead quiet. Not peaceful—just muffled, like the whole world had been told not to speak.

He trudged on, head swiveling frantically, right through wolf territory on his own. Every shadow in the tree line made him squint. Every cracked branch made his stomach jump.

Hours passed.

Finally, he reached her usual spot. The one near the frost-cracked stone where the Usnea grew thick.

Nothing.

No footprints. No drag marks. No shelter pit.

Just wind-whipped branches and a wide, bone-chilling hush.

River scanned the horizon, chest heaving. Then dropped to a crouch, removing his gloves and slicing his fingers into the snow. Cold bit his skin.

Seriously, Tamar…What were you thinking, going alone?

His hand closed around nothing but melting ice chips. He removed Duncan's snow shoes, letting himself sink into the cold fluff. Searching for hours with his hands and feet.

He stood again. Eyes narrowed.

She wasn't here. There was no sign of her.

But she *had* to be somewhere.

He should've protected her. Should've taken her for the Usnea.

Instead, he'd stood still. Just like he had before he…killed *that thing.*

Afraid of something he couldn't explain.

Something that lived in him, not out there.

He's not a monster—He'll find her and it will prove he's not.

Monsters don't get their greatest gifts back.

He scanned the endless white, cold light bleeding into the low clouds. A sinking dread pressed at his ribs.

She could be anywhere.

In the woods. Beyond the ridge. Buried under snow.

He took a slow breath. Snow shoes back on.

The White then.

Hours passed. Combing the path from there to the camp.

Still nothing.

No tracks. No signs. The storm had wiped the slate clean.

He started back, every step heavier than the last—until a faint figure appeared on the horizon. Wrong height. Wrong size. Wrong gait.

A man.

As River drew closer, relief loosened his chest. Big John had tracked him.

"Brought you food," he said, pulling jerky from his pack. "Duncan figured you weren't coming back to eat."

"Is everyone else still out?"

"The whole hunting team. A few sewers, too."

He handed River a long stick. "Use this. Storm hid everything. We could walk right over her."

River nodded, throat thick. She'd be hypothermic. "Thanks."

Big John gave his arm a firm pat. "We'll find her." Then he turned and vanished into the trees.

River pressed on. He called her name—once. Twice. Then quieter. His voice fell flat. The forest didn't echo right.

No answer.

The snow muted everything. As if it wanted her forgotten.

He paused by a narrow spruce, pressed his back to it. Ate slowly, numb fingers clumsy on the dried meat.

His eyes drifted. He forced them open again. *Keep going.*

She was out here. Somewhere.

He pushed deeper into the tree line. Dusk creeping in.

"Tamar!" he shouted again, louder than before. Desperate.

"Shhh!"

River spun towards the sound.

Takumi—half-hidden near a leaning evergreen, barely a shadow. His eyes locked on River with a blade sharp warning.

River gave him a one-raised brow look.

Takumi lifted a finger. "We're being tracked."

A long, low howl echoed behind him. Not far. Not near. Just... patient.

Wolves.

His body shivered, recalling his last encounter, when one tore into him during a late winter hunt. He placed a hand on his forearm scars. Few animals did he fear more—or respect.

"We're downwind," Takumi said quietly. "They'll keep on us, but wait for nightfall to move in."

River scanned the trees. "We're not making it back by dusk."

Takumi shook his head. "No."

"Then we face them."

"Face them?" Takumi shot him a look. "River, it's just us. We're not taking down a full pack."

"What if they get Tamar?"

Takumi's jaw tightened. "What if they already got Tamar?"

River's head snapped toward him, eyes flaring.

Takumi winced, voice softened. "I've been out here all day too. Just like you. I want to find her. But dying out here helps no one."

River exhaled hard. "So what do you suggest?"

"We double back on your trail. I'll dig out a shelter, you cover our backs. We hold the line until morning, take shifts on watch. They won't attack if they know we're alert. Not in our own den."

"And we just hope they give up?"

"They usually do."

"That depends how hungry they are. I can't leave Tamar out here."

"If she's still out here, she's in less danger than we are. That pack's tracking *us*."

"They might catch her scent."

"Possible. But less likely than her being home already, waiting for you."

River stood still for a beat, heart hammering as he tried to keep his fear at bay. "Fine," he muttered. "Your plan sucks, but I've got nothing better." He unslung his swords. "You lead. I'll cover rear."

They hustled back the way River had come, following his own snow-shoe marks. The snow clung heavy to their knees.

"It's going to be ridiculous trying to fight in snowshoes," River muttered.

"What choice do we have?"

"We're gambling hard on your theory that they won't attack before dark."

Takumi dropped to one knee and started clearing powdered snow with his arms. Beneath, the crusted layer packed tight. Good for cutting.

River kept his eyes on the tree line.

What if Takumi was wrong? What if the pack wasn't tracking—what if they were already circling?

Then—movement. A blur of shadow low and fast along the tree line.

He stiffened.

Takumi began slicing at the snow with a whale bone blade. River tossed him one of his steel swords.

"Thanks." Takumi plunged it in, carving out the first block.

"One down," he said. "Twenty-five more."

"We need fire."

"When we're under protection."

River glared, looking back at him. "A fire now would keep them back."

"*Turn back around!*" Takumi barked.

River spun, instinct snapping into place.

"Don't turn your back on them," Takumi hissed. "Hold your weapon out. Let them *see* it. Wolves are thinkers. They're measuring us. They attack when they know they can win."

Five blocks done. Takumi began curving the walls.

River risked a glance. "Didn't you lead the crew that wiped out the last pack?"

Takumi didn't look up. "Yeah."

River remembered that winter. Remembered the bodies.

And he remembered the dogs.

Takumi had come with two, family-trained, loyal to the bone. One died of age. The other, torn apart by a bear saving Takumi's life.

He never replaced them. Never got over it.

"How much longer?" River asked, voice low.

"Done by dusk." Takumi didn't pause his cutting. Six blocks down.

River's grip tightened on the sword. Shadows moved again at the edge of the trees. The wolves were getting restless. "How many did you say there were?"

"I don't think I did."

"I'm seeing five."

"It's probably less."

Teeth on edge, River kept watching. The blocks stacked higher. Ten. Eleven. Twelve. A shelter now, not just scattered slabs. Takumi carved fast, efficient, not wasting motion.

Then one of the wolves broke from the tree line.

It darted into the open, locked eyes with River. And retreated.

River didn't blink.

Takumi finished the last block. "Inside."

They crawled into the tight space, pressing into the cold. Takumi unwrapped a small lump of seal blubber, struck it with flint until it caught—slow, sputtering flame licking low. He pressed it against the base of the wall, sealing the inner edge as it melted a tight ring of ice. Cramped, but safe.

Finally, Takumi leaned back, exhaling. "You were hurt pretty badly from the last pack as I recall."

River nodded. "Like you said. They're smart."

"I'm surprised you're still alive."

"Took most of my ammo. I dropped one, but the others ran. My arm was slashed deep—I made it back, barely. If they'd gotten my legs, or if a polar bear had picked up the blood trail. .." He shrugged. "Would've been the end."

Takumi snorted. "And then I'd be Pack Leader."

River stared at him, silent.

Takumi looked away. "It's hard. Always being second. Knowing someone better will always be in your way."

"I'm not better than—"

"Spare me," he muttered. "Don't need your pity on top of everything else."

River kept watching him.

Takumi shifted in his seat.

How was he supposed to lead a man who held that kind of resentment for him?

How long had it been festering? And how long before it cracked open again?

Takumi's face softened. His shoulders dropped. For a long moment, he stared past River, eyes unfocused. "For what it's worth…" His voice was quiet. "I really hope we find her. I can't imagine the camp without her."

River nodded, barely. His bottom lip pulled inward. A silent thanks.

Takumi's bitterness—his yearning. It was almost like…

He couldn't bare the thought. The last thing he wanted to

do was ask it, but if he didn't, he'd be wondering his whole life. "Was there ever… anything between you and her?"

Takumi's eyes flicked back. He froze for a beat, then grinned wide with those annoying perfect teeth of his. That smug, knowing grin River hated.

Exactly why he hadn't wanted to ask.

"Not gonna lie, I thought about it." Takumi leaned back against the icy wall. "Many times. I would've been all for it."

River's fingers clenched around his sword hilt. If he killed him, would anyone know? He'd already killed one man before. Would another matter?

"…But she wouldn't have been. Not even close. She loved *you*. I don't know why. But it was you. All the way. And everyone knew it."

River swallowed hard.

Eyes glossy, with a hint of red underneath, Takumi glanced over. "You never deserved her."

"For once, Takumi, you and I are in complete agreement."

Takumi's voice cracked next. "She wasn't even some great beauty, you know? Not that she wasn't… but it wasn't that. It was how she *was*. She helped everyone. She was kind—to *everyone*." He paused, then laughed bitterly. "And not that fake kindness people put on when they want you to like them. Tamar loved people without agenda. Just… loved them."

His voice broke. Tears ran freely now. "How does someone like that even exist in a world like this?" He wiped at his face with a sleeve. "And now she's gone."

A silence settled.

River shifted into position by the entrance, blade ready. "I'll take first watch."

❧❄☙

Morning.

River woke to silence. The kind that made your stomach knot.

He crawled out, pulling his gun. Two bullets left. But the wolves were gone.

Just like Takumi said.

Paw prints scattered the snow around their shelter. Ghosts of the night before.

The men collected their things in silence. No words needed, leaving the shelter.

As they started to walk, River looked back and saw two wolves run out of the trees. "Incoming!"

They were too far from the shelter to make it back. No time.

The lead wolf stopped just beyond the rise, studying them as two more closed in behind it. Three wolves.

"We can take three," River muttered.

"Maybe," Takumi said, scanning the tree line. "But I counted four yesterday. Where's the fourth?"

River drew his handgun, two bullets left. Takumi nocked an arrow and let it fly. Missed. The second arrow veered too wide.

The wolves charged. River waited. Just a little closer.

Closer...

Then—movement to the east. A fourth wolf burst from the trees, cutting wide to flank.

Smart. Too smart.

Bam! Bam!

River dropped the leader and the second behind it in two clean shots. The flank wolf yelped. Takumi had caught it in the hind leg.

It skidded sideways, whimpering. The last one veered off and vanished into the trees.

Takumi approached the injured one, arrow still lodged in its leg. It whimpered again, not trying to bite, just watching.

“Are you going to put it out of its misery already?” River snapped, breathing hard.

Takumi crouched near it. “This isn’t a wolf.”

River frowned. “What do you mean it *isn’t a wolf?*”

“It’s a sled dog,” Takumi said quietly. “Must’ve gone wild after the Disaster. Fell in with a pack.”

River stared. “It tried to kill us.”

“Not because it's evil in some way. It's just hungry.” Takumi pulled a strip of dried meat from his pouch and held it out. The dog sniffed it, then began to chew, slow and cautious.

“See?” he said. “Maybe Laney can patch her up.”

River shook his head. “You’ve *got* to be kidding me. I need to get home. I need to know if Tamar made it back.”

“Then go. I’m taking this one.”

River hesitated. “Won’t it lead the rest back to us?”

“That pack already knows where we are.” Takumi met his eyes.

The animal didn’t growl. Just watched, quiet and trembling.

River sighed, jaw tight. He still thought it was a bad idea. But he didn’t feel like arguing.

They hiked in silence. The white stretched wide before them, cold and unyielding.

When the village finally came into view, River picked up his pace, stumbling, then running.

Down the snow-cut path, he shouted, voice cracking, “Tamar! Is she here?”

Duncan jogged toward him. “She’s not here, River.”

River’s heart dropped. “No one found her?”

“We searched all day yesterday,” Duncan said. “Half the hunting party’s back out now.”

River clutched his head, fell to his knees. Snow drifted around him.

No one found her.

Twelve

DAYS PASSED. THEN weeks.

Still no sign of her.

River searched every single day. Dawn to dusk. Through ice fog and knee-deep snow, he combed the same ridges and forest lines again and again—until even his own footprints seemed to mock him.

The hunting party gave up first. Quietly. Some of them had thought it was pointless from the beginning.

Rumors began to spread, whispers in small groups, that she'd wandered too far. Been blinded by the white. Fallen into the freezing water. That they'd never find her body.

River refused to believe it.

Even when logic gnawed at him. If she were alive, wouldn't she have made it back by now? And if she were injured… no food, no shelter this long—she'd be dead already.

Still, he packed up again one morning. Strapped his satchel tight. Reached for his bone skis—the ones Noah carved for him after the first week out.

Duncan caught his arm at the edge of the village. "How long are you going to do this?"

River didn't look at him. "As long as it takes."

"Your kids miss you."

"They miss their mother more." He turned away.

"River." Duncan's voice softened. "She's gone.

I miss her too. The whole village does. We need to mourn her before the winter move."

River's jaw flexed. He said nothing. Just scowled and pushed off into the snow.

❄

Another month passed. They should have moved by now. But held back because of him.

It was a huge risk he had forced on them.

The village held a memorial.

River stood near the back, stiff and silent, one hand on each of his children's shoulders. He didn't cry. Just stared across the ice horizon.

The women had collected dried primrose, saved from the short bloom, their petals pale and brittle but still fragrant. They wore fringes cut from softened hide, dyed green in remembrance for her favorite color. They tossed the flowers into the open tide pool beyond the ridge while Noah muttered a Christian prayer.

Even though she was Jewish.

She never talked about it much. Just said prayers quietly. Kept Sabbath to herself. The others didn't know, or didn't care to. They meant well—but they didn't know.

There was weeping. Moaning. Eerie, guttural wails rising from her closest friends.

Traditional Inuit mourning cries—raw, painful, unfiltered.

River joined them.

Didn't even think about it.

It just felt right. The only sound loud enough to carry

across the white.

The kind of sound the dead could hear.

The kind to let Tamar know how badly she was missed.

After it was over, River sat alone at the water's edge, watching the wind spin the primrose and other flowers in slow, aimless circles. Green dye bled from tassels flung into the shallows, painting streaks through the white foam

This was the day.

The anniversary.

And she couldn't be here for it.

The first time he could've celebrated it with her, was her funeral.

Duncan and Osha had taken the kids home without a word. Just a nod. Giving him space.

He didn't move when Ginger approached. Just kept staring at the water.

So she sat beside him.

No words. Just the sound of wind, waves, and mourning.

Eventually, he spoke, his eye red and glossy. "I never told her. Not really. Just how much I love her."

Ginger laid a hand on his shoulder. "She knew."

He watched her, eyes searching, watery. As if he needed her to mean it.

His fist came up to his mouth. He bit down hard, trying to hold it in.

"No—no, don't do that." She pulled him in, wrapping her hide blanket around both of them. "You can let it out. I won't tell anyone."

And he did.

The moment he had permission, the dam broke. His grief poured out of him—deep, guttural sobs that raked his chest and shook his shoulders. Ginger held him, arms firm around his back.

Even a man like River needed a place to fall apart.

She glanced over her shoulder—and saw Noah standing at

a distance, watching.

Her brow furrowed. What was he doing?

She raised a hand in a silent *what?*

Noah gave no answer. Just turned and walked away.

She pulled her coat tighter and gently rocked River where he leaned against her.

His breath started to steady. Slowly, he lifted his head, face blotched and tear-streaked.

"I don't know how I'm supposed to do this, Gin." His voice cracked. "How do I live without her?"

He turned back to the water. Wiped his face with his sleeve.

"You will," Ginger said softly. "Because you have to. Your kids need you. And Tamar would never want you to give up."

He shook his head, more in pain than protest.

"We'll help you through it," she said. "All of us." She reached for his arm. "It's getting late. We need to head back."

"You go on."

"No. I'm not leaving you here so you can throw yourself into the water."

"I wouldn't…"

"Come on," Ginger said gently. "There's a celebration in Tamar's honor."

River blinked. "A *what?*"

"Yeah. It's tradition the elders are bringing back. First, we mourn. Then we celebrate their passage into the next life."

He hesitated, but let her guide him.

Back at the main fire, the whole village had gathered. The flames danced high, casting long shadows. People made space for him without words, welcoming him in, folding him into warmth.

Ginger sat him down near the flames. Then stepped back, leaving him with his kids, standing beside Noah—but her eyes stayed on River.

Jason handed him a carved bone cup filled with moonshine. River took it, but didn't drink. Just stared into the fire, his eyes red and swollen.

Stories began to rise.

Laney spoke first. She told of Tamar's uncanny knowledge of plants—how she could smell a fever before the symptoms showed. How she never hesitated to share what she knew.

Big John followed. He remembered a night when the cold bit through his clothing, and Tamar had silently slipped her extra coat over his shoulders. Always giving. Always watching out for others.

Ginger's voice was soft. "She was my friend. My *real* friend. I don't know who I'll talk to now."

Duncan spoke last. "A devoted mother. And fierce about it. She loved those kids like breath in her lungs. And her love for River…" He glanced toward him. "I've seen a lot of couples. But hers was the rare kind—the kind that didn't stop, even when it hurt."

River flinched and started to rise, wanting to retreat to the safety of his home, but Big John and Jason each laid a hand on his shoulders, pressing him gently back down.

He didn't fight them.

Just sat.

Exhausted. Hollowed out.

Across the fire, Duncan raised his cup. "To Tamar."

The whole circle echoed it. "*To Tamar!*"

They drank.

River stared at his cup.

Then—wordlessly—he drank too.

The men whooped. Ginger gave a small smile, watching from the shadows.

Jason refilled River's cup.

He drank again.

And again.

Each one blurring the edges. Softening the ache.

For a little while, it didn't hurt quite so much.

After the fourth, his body slumped. The world tilted.

River dropped back into the snow, out cold.

Takumi and Big John moved quickly, lifting him between them. Ginger followed, steadying them, pulling open the flap to his home.

Inside, they laid him on his bed. Ginger knelt to pull off his boots and wrap him in a thick hide blanket. "I hope we did the right thing," she said quietly.

Takumi stepped back toward the door. "He's not going to think so in the morning."

Ginger lingered, blowing out the lamp.

She watched River's sleeping for a long moment before stepping outside.

Poor guy.

Everyone knew how much he loved her.

Tonight wasn't about forgetting. They just wanted to give him room to breathe.

TAMAR FOUND THE Usnea lichen exactly where it had been last year—clinging to the northern side of a frost-split log beneath a canopy of evergreens.

She crouched low, fingers moving fast, stuffing the fibrous tufts into her satchel.

A sharp *huff* broke the stillness.

Her breath caught.

That was the sound of a horse.

They didn't have horses up here. Not since before the moon.

Slowly, she lifted her head.

A brown horse stood just beyond the clearing. Atop it—a man.

He wasn't from her camp.

She hadn't seen another soul outside her people since before her trip to the moon. The strangeness of a new face hit her hard. Curious.

And afraid.

He didn't speak. Just watched.

Something in his face unsettled her. Not open. Not kind.

She kept her hand steady as best she could, yanking the last of the lichen free. Don't panic. Don't react.

Maybe he's just startled too.

She slowly unsheathed her knife where he couldn't see. Once her bag was full, she slung it over her shoulder, turned her back to him, and walked away.

Don't run. Not yet.

A second *huff* behind her. Then hooves.

A rope caught her clean across the shoulders, jerking her off her feet.

She hit the ground hard, air punched from her chest. Duststung her eyes.

All right then.

The rope bit into her arms, cinched tight around her chest. He thought she was just some woman gathering plants . Harmless.

He had no idea who she was.

She didn't fight yet. Just lay still. Face to the horizon.

*Let him come close.*Think three moves out.

She heard him dismount. Gravel crunched under his boots.

Closer.

Closer.

She whipped her head back and *slammed* it into his nose.

He yelped, stumbling back, hands flying to his face.

He came at her, mouth pressed, blood from the nose dripping down his chin.

She ducked his first swing, drove her foot into his gut. He

Tamar rolled to her side and kicked her legs free of the slack in the rope, twisting fast. She was on her feet before he recovered, fists up, knife ready, weight balanced. grunted, doubled slightly—but not enough.

Too big. Too fast.

He recovered quick, grabbed her by the arm and flung her into a tree trunk. Bark tore into her shoulder. She spun, gasping and landed a heel into his knee with a scream. He staggered again, limping.

Don't stop.

She launched herself forward, teeth bared, ready to take out his throat if she had to.

But he caught her mid-charge. Why did she attack?

"You got cocky!" River said, in her head.

The man lifted her clean off the ground and threw her down.

Air left her lungs in a crackling gasp. Her vision blurred.

Before she could find her bearings, he straddled her back and yanked her arms behind her, taking her knife.

She kicked, thrashed, spat curses. He said nothing.

Thick cord bound her wrists. Her elbows. Then her ankles.

Still silent, still methodical.

She screamed into the dirt as he hoisted her up, put a bag over her head and slung her on the back of his horse like a sack of gear.

The lichen she was gathering scattered to the ground with the bag—forgotten.

She lifted her head once as the horse started moving, biting the bag to turn it to the one bit of light she could see through a hole. Trees blurred past.

She didn't even know which direction was home anymore.

But she memorized the back of his coat.

She would get free.

And when she did—*she'd finish the fight.*

Continued to Fault Lines…

Thank you for reading Aftershocks.

This book wasn't backed by a giant publisher.
No marketing machine. No corporate push.
Just a story. And readers.

If you enjoyed it, the most powerful thing you can do is leave a review. A single paragraph can change everything for an indie author.

Thank you for being part of this journey.

Get additional cut scenes, and updates on future publications by subscribing at:
https://authorerinwilkerson.com/
*Merch available for purchase

https://linktr.ee/Erin__Wilkerson

A special *Thank You* to these

Bookstagram accounts!

So much wouldn't have been possible without you.

Emsi Sage @sagieewrites

Melody Kepler @melodykepler.writer

Meredith @meredithsbooknook

Tiffany Marie Ticer @readingmom_era

Chloeey @theenrichmentoffiction1

Debbie H Kaiah @debbie.kaiah

Dani @danii_reads_

Josh White @joshwhitebooks

Follow them for the

best bookish content!

This story draws inspiration from traditional Inuit survival practices, material culture, and values surrounding community and respect for the land. While this is a work of fiction set in a speculative world, I am deeply grateful for the history and knowledge preserved by Inuit communities.

Any errors are my own.

Selected Sources

- The Tuktu documentary series, on YouTube produced by the National Film Board of Canada.
- Morrison, David. 2004. Inuit Culture. In The Oxford Companion to Canadian History. Gerald
- Hallowell, ed. Oxford: Oxford University Press.
- LeMoine, Genevieve. 2003. Woman of the House: Gender, Architecture, and Ideology in Dorset Prehistory. Arctic Anthropology 40(1): 121–138.
- McElroy, Ann. 1975. Canadian Arctic Modernization and Change in Female Inuit Role
- Identification. American Ethnologist 2(4): 662–686.
- Rowan, Mary Caroline (2014).Co-constructing early childhood programs nourished by Inuit worldviews, Études/Inuit/Studies. 38 (1–2): 73–94. doi:10.7202/1028854ar ISSN 0701 1008.
- Guemple, David L. "The Role of Gender in Traditional Inuit Society." Études/Inuit/Studies 10, no.1–2 (1986): pages.

About the author

"Erin Wilkerson is a writer of YA fantasy and science fiction stories, which often feature fierce, comedic, and sassy female characters ready to take on the world and kick butt. She aspires to hole up somewhere with her manuscripts, writing in isolation for hours, but there is no way that'll ever happen since she is the proud ringleader of this traveling troupe of rambunctious monkeys. Life swallows up her time, but it makes for hilarious stories to share with her readers. She resides in Texas with her circus."

-- Written by close friend and fellow author Esra Morwood